Life
Surprises

Life

Surprises

SEVEN SHORT STORIES
ABOUT THE UNEXPECTED

by
John W. Sloat

CCB Publishing
British Columbia, Canada

Life Surprises: Seven Short Stories About the Unexpected

Copyright ©2012 by John W. Sloat
ISBN-13 978-1-77143-014-2
First Edition

Library and Archives Canada Cataloguing in Publication
Sloat, John W., 1932-
Life Surprises : seven short stories about the unexpected / by John W. Sloat – 1st ed.
ISBN 978-1-77143-014-2
Also available in electronic format.
Additional cataloguing data available from Library and Archives Canada

Cover artwork: White seagull feather: © Zts | Dreamstime.com
Beautiful seascape: © Veronika Vasilyuk | Depositphotos.com

Publisher: CCB Publishing
               British Columbia, Canada
               www.ccbpublishing.com

Other Books by John W. Sloat

Lord, Make Us One, 1986
The Other Half, 2001
Memories of My Misadventures, 2008
A Handbook For Heretics, second edition, 2009
Moving Beyond the Christian Myth, 2011

Contents

I

The Feather

I: Emily

When I was a little girl, almost seven years old, Mommy and I spent a week at the beach in North Carolina. It was a special extravagance since money was tight at that point in her life. Of course, I didn't know anything about that, since she carefully kept it from me. All I knew was that Daddy didn't live with us anymore.

The light seemed to have gone with him when he left the house, and we both experienced long, lonely days. We didn't talk about it, at least not much, and as a result there were frequent echoing silences between us. But we were best friends, and Daddy's absence drew us even closer.

So it was a great thrill when Mommy said we were going to spend a week at the ocean. She had grown up in New Jersey, and had often talked about how wonderful it was to swim in the ocean. She told me stories about the fun she and her brother had had at places like Cape May and Seaside Heights and Atlantic City. But for some reason, we never quite got there. The promises, mostly from Daddy, were always, "Maybe next year."

Now that Daddy was gone, Mommy suddenly said, "Definitely this year." Despite my young age, I knew what a big event this was going to be for her, and I was sure it would

1

be a shaft of light in the darkness we had been sharing for months.

When Daddy left, we had to give up our house in Minnesota and move to Norfolk, Virginia, where my grandmother lived. As a result, instead of going to one of Mommy's New Jersey beaches, she said we were going to the Outer Banks. It didn't matter to me where we went, of course, so long as I could swim in the ocean.

We moved into a little house on the beach on a Saturday afternoon. It was a week after the end of first grade and I was about to turn seven, so our trip was sort of an early birthday present. Back in those days, my mother was able to afford a place right on the beach, something that would be impossible today. But our house backed up to the dunes, and a little boardwalk led from our backyard right out onto the sand.

My jaw dropped when I first caught sight of the ocean. I had never imagined so much water, never been aware of the horizon before. I asked, "Is that where the Earth ends?" and kept bombarding her with questions – "How far does the water go?" Answer: To our old house and back. "Why is the water all crashy and bumpy like that?" Answer: That's called surf. You can go play in it. "What's that smell?" Answer: That's salt, because the ocean is salty.

As soon as we got things situated in the cottage, we went to the beach. It was a glorious day, and I was torn between dancing in the water and playing in the sand. Mommy helped me build my first sandcastle, and held my hand so I could practice jumping over the waves as they came up on the shore to die. We played for the rest of the afternoon, and I had never felt the sun so close or enjoyed the outdoors so passionately. The sounds of the gulls squawking overhead, the constant crash of the waves, the caress of the ocean breeze, the feel of the sand under my feet, everything was exaggerated until I was overwhelmed by the immensity of it all. A million times I said to Mommy, "This is so much *fun!*"

When supper was over, I dragged her back to the beach. She said that it was too cold to swim anymore, but that we could play in the sand until it got dark. I decided that if we couldn't go into the water, we would bring the water up to us. So, with Mommy's help, I dug a long ditch straight toward the water, hoping that the waves would fill it and create a tiny canal right up to where we had spread our blanket.

Our lives are divided into sections, and we tend to label those sections by saying that they happened before or after such-and-such an event. But nothing warns us that the actual event is about to happen, that this moment is the final word in one whole paragraph of our life.

Mommy was digging her part of the ditch down near the water, and I had wet down a patch of sand higher up so I could dig the opposite end of the ditch. We were about ten or twelve feet apart.

I didn't see him coming, but suddenly a man walked between us. I was hunched down concentrating on my work, so I didn't notice much of anything about him except that he seemed to be tall. I glanced up as he spoke to me, but later could remember only blue shorts and dirty white sneakers.

He didn't stop and talk to me. He merely slowed as he walked by. "Here," he said, "you need a feather." And then he was gone. I didn't actually see him leave because I was focused on the feather.

Since he passed by five or six feet away, he didn't hand me the feather. He simply let it go and a gentle breeze off the ocean took it from him and dropped it right alongside me. I picked it up and looked at it, but when I turned to search for him, he was at some distance, beginning to merge with others on the beach.

I heard my mother say, "Oh, a feather!" as she came over to examine it. It was about six inches long, perfectly formed and intact, and pure white except for a slight tinge of blue-gray color along its narrow side. It was beautiful, not the least bit soiled, and looked…new. I turned it over and was fascinated by the fine detail, the way the barbs interlocked, their diminishing length as they neared the tip, and the fuzz at the bottom of the stem. "It's so light," I said, bouncing it in my hand.

Mommy smiled. "Did you ever hear someone say, as light as a feather?" I nodded as the meaning of that familiar statement sank in.

I looked back down the beach because of a lingering curiosity about the man who had appeared and then disappeared so quickly, but he had vanished into the evening mist. I planted the feather like a flag at the end of our sandy canal, and it served as a target for the water which never did fill our little ditch. Eventually, we let go of our first day at the ocean and climbed into bed. My beautiful white feather was tucked under the edge of an old framed black-and-white photo of the ocean above my bed. As I looked up at it during the night, it seemed to glow in the light from the streetlamp.

I don't remember what we did during the rest of that week, but I do recall watching people go by and hunting for my mysterious feather-man. I never did see him again or, if I did, I couldn't recognize him. But his gift became the focus of my visit to the ocean. I carried my feather with me wherever we went, showing it to anyone who seemed interested, and repeating the story of how it came to me.

It was inevitable, given my fascination with my treasure, that we should start inventing stories about the shadowy man who had crossed my path for less than ten seconds. Maybe he was a beachcomber whose hobby was looking for treasures to share with others. Perhaps he was a ghost from some pirate ship who was doomed to wander the shores and then vanish. Or he might be a Professor of Feathers who spent his summers adding to his collection, before going back to some obscure college in the fall to lecture about them.

Then, as an afterthought, my mother came up with the idea that stuck in my heart like an arrow in a bullseye – "Maybe he was your guardian angel." The shock of recognition which followed that offhand statement made me certain it was true, that she had figured it out.

"My guardian angel." I said the words dozens of times that night, feeling the taste and the shape of them on my tongue. *My guardian angel.* The sound of that phrase gave me a whole new sensation – safety, peace. I realize now that after the months of uncertainty, of losing my home and worrying about what might happen next, I was looking for something to give me back my security. And this was it.

Later, I recalled what the man had said when he delivered my gift – "Here, you need a feather." I mentioned it to my mother who thought about it for a moment and then said, "That was strange. He could have said, 'Here's a feather,' or 'Do you want a feather?' I wonder why he would say, 'You *need* a feather.'"

At the end of the week, we went back to our new home, my new school, and a different life. And as that life progressed, I was aware that I was being companioned by unseen forces, guarded by an invisible presence no farther away than the gust of wind which had carried the feather from his hand to mine. And I knew it was all true because I had proof; I possessed a tangible talisman that, at least to my mind, banished all doubt. I had my own personal guardian angel who had once walked within arm's reach of me. In time, everyone knew my story, all the kids in my class, all the members of my family – I was the girl with the guardian angel. Well, everyone has a guardian angel, presumably, but I had *seen* mine.

I wouldn't say the feather was an obsession, but it certainly helped define who I was. It connected me with heaven, with my childhood, with the North Carolina shoreline, and it gave me a dimension of serenity which I noticed was missing in many of my friends.

As the years passed, however, I talked less and less about it. All the important people in my life already knew the story, and I had learned the hard way that repeating it once too often brought less than tolerant responses. But more than that, it was such a personal part of who I was that I no longer wanted to share it. It somehow helped organize my core self, it gave my life a kind of private mystical dimension.

That peace at the core of my being helped me get through my high school years in a system where to have little was to be little. It got me though college, where graduating with the limited means my mother could afford often meant working at two jobs in addition to my classes. It also meant staying an extra year because I was sick one summer, couldn't work, and had no money for the fall term. It served me through my internship as a physician's assistant on a staff where jealousy and favoritism tried their hardest to make me fail. And it surrounded and supported me through an ill-advised marriage, the loss of a baby, and a divorce that took most of what little I had left.

While I tried to put my life back together, a strange idea began to form in my subconscious. My feather had been an absolutely essential icon in my life. It had led me back into the church, and I had attached it to the front flyleaf of the Bible which I always had with me. It made God, or at least my angel, a present and active part of every day of my life.

But at the same time, I began to realize that that feather had taken on an almost magical character; the symbol had become

6

as important to me as the divine presence which it represented. I gradually came to see that this was immature, that it bordered on idolatry. That realization came to me in an odd way.

I babysat for my cousin's little girl one night. Her name was Amy and she was four. We were very close, and I tried to spend time with her as often as possible. It was about a year after I lost my baby, and that made our bond even more emotional.

She loved the Disney film *Dumbo*, and that night she begged me to watch it with her. I had never seen *Dumbo* before, which shows how deprived my childhood had been! Watching it for the first time that night was a revelation for me. When Timothy Mouse picked a feather out of the crow's tail and handed it to Dumbo, I was amused but didn't make the connection. Then, at the climax of the movie, when Dumbo is in his powerdive clutching his black feather, something began to register. And the instant it slipped from his trunk, I felt a cold shock over my whole body. *He had lost his feather!* I knew exactly how he felt – the terror, the loss, the emptiness. Then it came crashing in on me – *I was Dumbo!*

It's hard to describe the breadth of the realization that spread over me. It wasn't that I had made an idol of the feather. And it wasn't even that I was looking on my guardian angel as a kind of magic cloak protecting me from harm and disappointment. It was that life doesn't rely for success on magic feathers or guardian angels, or even faith in God. All of those things are outside of me. Rather, it has to do with my core, the very heart of me for which I had always given credit to my angel. But that power had always been inside of *me*; my angel, my wonderful angel, had been my own courage and determination all those years.

And in that instant, I knew what I had to do to purge myself of all my years of magic thinking. I had to find my angel, my feather-giver from so many years ago. I laughed aloud as I heard myself arrive at that conclusion. What was the likelihood that I could find him after all this time? One in a million? One in a billion? How could I even be sure he was still alive? I had no idea how old he was when I first caught a glimpse of him. To a child, a sixteen-year-old can look like an old man. I was now thirty: it had been twenty-three years since that summer when I was just turning seven.

But I knew I had to try. And I knew how to do it. The Internet. It became a sudden all-consuming passion, and I couldn't wait to get started. I wrote out the story in as much detail as I could, trying to identify time and place so as to make it as recognizable to my "angel" as possible. I told him how incredibly important his tiny act of kindness had been in my life. And I explained why I wanted to find him, not just to thank him but in a sense to get him out of my system, to close the circle which had been gradually forming for almost a quarter century.

I launched the site on New Year's Day, thinking that the symbolic date might give me a little better chance of success. I pleaded with the readers to spread the word, to help me get as much coverage for my story as possible. Then I sat back and waited, praying for the greatest miracle of all in my unlikely story.

But, of course, nothing happened. I kept checking the site to make sure it was working properly. Months went by. A few responses trickled in, but they were mostly comments about the story or suggestions as to how I could find my man. Then I got responses from two different people the same day saying that my search was over, that each of them had given me the feather. My heart sank. Even with all the work I had done to set up the site, I never really expected to find the man. But if I was going to have to sort through a bunch of phonies, how could I make sure I didn't miss the real person in the process? That was something I hadn't considered.

Then, in June, something amazing happened. Within one week, two established websites picked up my story, and days later it was all over the Internet. In fact, it became something of a *cause célèbre*. With this kind of coverage, my hopes began to soar. *Newsweek* even picked it up for a brief human interest article and I began to be inundated with email. It seemed that everybody knew someone who might/could/should be or definitely was my man. And I had dozens of letters from him, or at least people purporting to be him. But none of them rang true. There were proposals of marriage, people claiming to have given me feathers on a hundred different beaches, even two women who said they were the person I was looking for but explaining that they had been disguised as men on that long-ago day.

And then it all quit. Just dropped off to a trickle, no more than a few each week, and still nothing definitive. I left the site up but ignored it more and more, rarely checking the mail. January came again and I reexamined the odds I had confronted a year ago at the beginning of the quest. They were way too long – I was just being silly. Maybe he really was an angel and had no access to email! I thought about taking the site down.

And then in May, almost a year and a half after I had launched the site, I finally heard from him.

✝ ✝ ✝ ✝ ✝ ✝ ✝ ✝ ✝ ✝ ✝ ✝ ✝

II: Thomas

That year was one to forget. It was something like a breach of contract. Things go wrong in everyone's life, but you aren't supposed to lose everything, especially not if you're working for the Big Guy.

I'd put in thirty-four years in four different parishes, and had quit at age fifty-nine, totally burned out. People didn't want to hear the truth any more. Serving a congregation had degenerated into a gun battle between your own principles and the people who wanted to run you and the church, people who had totally forgotten that the whole point of the exercise was to act like Christ in your daily life. Pastors were not spiritual counselors anymore, they were more like corporate managers where the focus was on budgets and sucking up to the clients.

That wasn't what I had signed on for. I guess I still had some childish illusion coming out of Princeton Seminary that I could make a difference, that I could become a change agent, that my parishes might just possibly begin to resemble little outposts of the Kingdom. I graduated in the middle of World War II, but was excused from service because of a rheumatic heart. Our son had been born a year earlier, and we set off with high hopes to a small charge in the boonies of eastern Tennessee.

I worked my way up through 200- and 600-member congregations until I became co-pastor of a 2,500-member church in Charlotte, North Carolina. At each stop, I laid all my high-falootin' ideas on them about Stewardship, caring for the least and the lost, and they always mollified me by nodding their heads during the sermon. But then at a board meeting at that last place, they voted to ignore the least and the lost and go into debt for $50,000 so they could install an elevator for the benefit of three rich old members. After a while, it felt like being an accomplice to an ongoing crime. So I got out.

But God can be a hostile old employer. I can't imagine that He was in favor of that kind of ecclesiastical self-interest, but just try to drop out in protest and you'll see how fast the axe falls. Within a month, because I had to give up my church-owned housing, my wife and I were living in a used trailer on the back forty of a farm owned by a friend in the congregation. Within six months, my financial advisor declared bankruptcy and told me that my investments were worth about 10% of what I had given him, so I didn't even have the money to sue him. A couple of months after that, I developed atrial fibrillation, spent a week in the hospital and had my insurance cancelled. And nine months later, my wife and thirty-year-old son, Donny, were killed in a car crash.

I had lost everything in this world that meant anything to me. But that wasn't enough for God. After this last disaster, He finished me off by taking the one thing I had left: my faith. I was working part-time in two churches as a Minister of Visitation, trying to stay off welfare, and one day found myself calling on an old lady who had just lost her husband. I listened to myself talking to her, and suddenly realized that I didn't believe anything I was saying. It was all just empty words, theological crap that kept people from thinking, from discovering the terrible truth – God couldn't care less about us. We're on our own. There is no mercy, no love, no reward for good behavior, no hope of a glorious future, nothing but empty words, empty beliefs, empty tomorrows.

Three days later, my farmer friend banged on the door of the trailer to ask what was the matter. He hadn't seen me since Sunday and thought I might be sick. What he found appalled him. I was unshaven, unbathed, undressed, unfed and deep in depression. So, being the take-charge type, he went to work. Within days, I had been to the doctor's, was on anti-depression medication, and was off to his cottage on the Outer Banks. I walked up and down the waterline for hours, listening to the surf, smelling the saltwater, and asking myself why it wouldn't be easier just to turn east and keep walking.

I had never stayed at the ocean before, and I gradually discovered why my friend had sent me there. It was just before the regular season so there weren't too many people around. Sitting and watching the endless motion of the waves and listening to the mesmerizing sound of the surf began to ease my black mood. Somehow, hours of walking became my therapy, and by the end of the week I was feeling a little less desperate.

I began to think about what was left of my family. My wife was gone. So was my son. His six-year-old twins had moved to California with their mother, my daughter-in-law, who was in real estate. Her atheistic ideas had always been a barrier between us, to which she had now added the additional barrier of the continent. My daughter, Ginger, lived in Maryland. She and Herm had married late and, though she was thirty-two, she was only now expecting her first baby.

There were no children for me to interact with anymore, now that my daughter was grown and Don's twins were out of reach. I had not been prepared for the way in which children leave your life as you get older. I saw families here and there on the beach introducing their little ones to the surf and the sand, and I felt a mild kind of envy at their good fortune. Did they realize how lucky they were? Did they appreciate how beautiful children were, what a blessing it was to be able to care for and teach them, to spend time with them, what joy it was to feel their hugs and share their kisses?

The next day I would have to pack up and go back to my routine. What had changed? Nothing. How was a week on the Outer Banks supposed to solve anything? Life just had nothing left to offer at this stage. There was only more of the same, day after day, until one merciful morning I wouldn't wake up.

After supper, I decided to take one final walk up the beach. By this time, I knew the shoreline pretty much by heart –

where you had to walk at high tide to keep your feet dry, when it was safe to walk at the water's edge. I even began to recognize some of the people, especially the little ones who had been there for most of the week. That was one of the reasons for walking, to see the children. Children could still warm the dark empty place that was my heart.

Since that week was the first time I'd ever stayed at the beach, I'd had no experience in shelling. So to help pass the time, I had collected some unusual shells during the previous six days. I stored them in a couple of old bean cans on a shelf in the kitchen, but I knew they had no place back home. They would only remind me of the fleeting pleasure of that week gone by and of the fact that nothing had changed. So I emptied the cans into my pockets, took the shells with me, and ceremonially threw them all back into the ocean, as though I was scattering the ashes of some old friend.

I kept walking, reluctant to end my final visit to the ocean, quite certain that I would never see it again. But I couldn't break the habit of looking down for shells – and that is when I saw the feather. Throughout that entire week, I hadn't seen a single feather lying on the beach. But now there was one at my feet. I didn't plan to pick it up because I was through collecting things, but the tide was coming in and the feather was going to be washed away. Also, it looked pristine, as though it had never been used, even by the bird who shed it. So I picked it up. It was pure white except for a hint of bluish gray along one edge. Not sure what I was going to do with it, I stuck it in the band of my hat.

I walked to the breakwater which had been the limit of my northward wanderings, then turned back toward the cottage. My mind was now on packing and making the long trip back to Charlotte, to a future I didn't anticipate with pleasure.

It was then that I first caught sight of her. It surprised me a little because there were two of them on a portion of the beach which had been uninhabited all week. They appeared to be a mother and daughter, and I stopped because in a few steps I would be past them; something about the scene made me want to extend the moment.

It was a lovely sight, the two of them on their knees working on some joint project, the mother nearer the water, the little girl higher up on the beach industriously shoveling sand. The girl was wearing a light blue bathing suit with a frilly skirt, and was facing my direction. I knelt in the sand, pretending to look for shells, hoping to be less noticeable. The mother had her back to me and was intent on making some kind of large hole in the wet sand.

The little girl – about six or seven years old – had masses of curly strawberry blond hair. The sun, low in the western sky, lit her hair from the rear so that it absolutely glowed. She looked like a tiny angel, beautiful beyond description. When I couldn't delay any longer, I rose and walked toward them, trying to get a clear view of her face. But she was looking downward, putting the finishing touches on some sort of ditch which ran clear down to the water where her mother was working. Studying her as I approached, I focused on her profile and her hair, ablaze with the setting sun.

As I reached the point where they were kneeling, I noticed her right shoulder blade. It appeared and disappeared as she worked her shovel, like a tiny wing slowly waving back and forth. She *is* an angel, I thought to myself, an unfledged baby angel. And at that moment I thought of the feather in my hat. I held it out toward her and dropped it as I said, "Here, you need a feather."

But instead of falling to the sand, the feather caught a breeze and wafted gently to her side, landing by her knee. She looked up briefly as I stepped across the ditch they were digging, and then she picked up the feather and looked at it. I desperately wanted to stay, but I was afraid the mother would think I was acting inappropriately around her child. As I moved beyond them, I heard the mother say, "A feather!" I looked back once and saw the two of them studying it, but they had their backs to me and that was the last I saw of them.

I couldn't get the vision of that little girl out of my mind, though. She inhabited my dreams that night and I woke thinking about her, wondering if I might catch one more glimpse of her before I left. I drove down to the same place the next morning, walked through someone's yard and searched the beach, but it was deserted. She was gone. One more loss, and I was a little surprised at the pain I felt knowing that I would never see her again.

Eventually, I moved in with my daughter, Ginger, in Maryland. Herman, her husband, was a sales manager for Allis Chalmers and was gone most weeks. So I provided company for her and helped out around the house when Herm was gone. I had always been able to talk to Ginger about the deeper things of life. She had been raised in my churches, of course, but had never really believed any of the things she heard me saying from the various pulpits. She had always been a doubter, a free thinker, someone with the depth to formulate her own beliefs about the spiritual world.

She had recently gotten into new age thinking, and we often had conversations late into the night in which she wondered how I could still hold to my old ideas about God. She listened as I struggled through the pain of my lost faith. I was in mortal agony, but she kept assuring me that my pain was therapeutic. It wasn't exactly what I wanted to hear, but she was certain I would come out on the other side a new man.

Ginger's pregnancy was proceeding well, and we were excited about the prospect of a new baby, her first, my third grandchild. Later that fall, about a month after I moved in, Ginger had a sonogram and found out that the baby was a girl. She was due around Christmas. We often spoke about the baby, imagining her future and suggesting names for her. Like all mothers-to-be, Ginger spent a lot time shopping for little girl things, and the baby became a real and tangible member of our family long before she made her appearance. Herm and I developed little rituals of patting Ginger's expanding tummy and talking to the baby whom, in the absence of an official name, we called Angel.

One night, sitting around the kitchen table, Ginger and I got to talking about my loss of faith again, and she used the image of a snake for me, which I thought a bit unflattering. She told me that I had to shed my old theology, to wriggle out of the hard shell of my calcified ideas and discover a new me in a smooth, fresh skin. She promised that when I went through this process, the lights would come on again, and that some event would trigger it.

I thought about that idea for a long moment, and then started to tell her about my time at the beach. I hadn't talked about it before because most of that week had been spent wandering aimlessly up and down, out of touch with everyone, even as I watched families enjoying their connectedness. For a whole week, I never spoke to another soul.

Except for that one moment.

I pondered whether or not to tell her the story. There was really nothing to it – I had picked up a feather, given it to a little girl, and walked on. But there was another reason I hadn't shared the story with anyone. That insignificant little speck of time in my sixty years had taken on an importance way out of proportion to its reality. I felt foolish telling anyone about my love for a little girl whom I had encountered for less than a minute, whose voice I had never heard, whose face I had not really seen. It was too delicate a memory to trust anyone else with.

After mulling it over for a bit, I said to Ginger, "I think I may have experienced that trigger event you were talking about." God bless her, she listened to my story with real sympathy and understanding, and she even teared up as I talked about the halo of strawberry blond hair lit by the sun, the tiny shoulder blade, and the passing comment, "You need a feather." There was a long silence, and then she whispered, "If you can feel all that, you can find your way back to the light again. And maybe that's why your little angel was there at that moment, to show you the way."

The months passed and December came. On the 20th, less than a week before Christmas, Ginger gave birth to her little girl, and our lives changed dramatically. Our pre-natal adoration of this tiny person apparently had a lasting effect, because Ginger and Herm named her Angela.

As the baby grew and was less reliant on her mother, I did more and more of the babysitting. Angela was a healthy child who laughed a lot and brought an incredible amount of sunshine into our home. She had been born with quite a bit of straight brownish hair, but by her first birthday it had turned curly and strawberry blond!

Angela was the perfect name for her. She was happy, curious, tolerant of all our adoring nonsense, willing to go to anyone, perfectly at home in the world. Yet, there was also a kind of solemn depth to her that was unusual in a little kid, a profound knowing that could be seen in her eyes. It was like she harbored some special wisdom and was merely waiting until she developed speech to share it with us.

When Ginger went back to work part-time after Angela's first birthday, I ended up doing even more of the babysitting. I had been given an opportunity to be a parent again, and it made a huge difference in my attitude. She was a gift from heaven who could unlock the pearly gates, even for an old pagan like me. You couldn't watch her without believing in God.

My conversations with Ginger steered my thinking in the direction of new age ideas. I read all the stuff she recommended, and after a while it began to make sense. It was a way back into the divine presence that avoided all the rubbish I had been taught in seminary. But then the memories would come rushing back in, and I would remember that God was either an illusion or the devil in disguise.

I became Angela's primary sitter when she started school. I would take her to the bus, meet her at the end of the day, sit with her while she had her after-school snack, listen to her while she debriefed, and help her with her homework. I taught her to play the piano and we studied Spanish together. Everyone talked about G-pa's angel. She had invented that nickname for me because, as she said, it saved time, words and ink. Family and friends were aware of this special connection between the oldest and youngest members of the clan. There was something charming and inspirational about it.

One day, when she was about seven, we were sitting on the back porch after school talking about deep matters. She had always been able to hold her own in a serious discussion, and often had something startling and insightful to offer. We got to talking about angels and she asked me if I believed in them. I said I wasn't sure. She looked at me, perplexed, and said, "Well, they believe in you." I had to smile.

"Do you think they're real?" I asked.

She looked at me as though I was a child who needed some basic instruction. "If God is real," she said, "then angels have to be real. You *do* believe in God?" I could hardly keep from laughing. She was so grownup and I loved her so much.

"I used to," I told her. "I used to tell people about God

every Sunday. But now I'm not so sure what I believe."

She pushed out her lips and wrinkled her nose, hunting for the proper response to someone like me, someone who should know better than to think such silly thoughts. "Well, I came from God. Do you believe in *me*?" I burst out laughing. It was like she was gazing into my soul. "Well, do you?"

She had me. "Of course I do," I confessed.

"Well," she went on, "I'm your angel, so you've seen me. And you once told me that you had seen another angel. I don't know anyone else who has actually seen a real angel. Tell me that story again." She already knew it well, but something in her seven-year-old mind knew that retelling it would be therapeutic for me, might even ease my doubts.

So I told her the story again. This time, she was even more excited about the similarities between herself and that nameless little angel in the sand – their strawberry blond hair, the fact that I called them both my angel, and the realization that she was now the same age as that other little girl had been. We pondered the images for a while, and then she said, "I wonder what she's doing now. Right now. Do you ever wonder about that?"

I nodded. "All the time."

Angela asked, "How old do you think she is now?"

"Well, if she was seven when I saw her and you were born almost a year later, and you're now seven, that would make her fifteen."

She shook her head. "Wow!" she whispered softly. After a moment, she switched subjects. "You know," she said, "I was your angel even before I was born."

I looked at her in surprise. "You were?"

"Yes," she went on. "I used to watch you to make sure you didn't get into trouble."

I raised my eyebrows. "You did?"

19

"Yep," she concluded with a sharp nod of her head. Then, her timing perfect, she added slowly, "And you needed a lot of watching!"

The years go faster the older you get, so even this new generation of children grew up and got away from me. Soon, Angela didn't need babysitting any longer and I was unemployed again. But our bond was very tight, and she made time to sit and talk almost every day. And when we spoke, that other child often seemed to stand just behind her in the shadows. "How old is Angel now?" she would ask every few months, perfectly able to do the calculations herself. The formula was always the same – "If she was eight when you were born, she would now be twenty-three." And Angela would always respond with a soft "Wow!"

She graduated from Dartmouth with a magna cum laude degree in math, and went to work as a designer for a software company in New England. She was on her way to an independent and successful career, and we were all very proud of her. But she still called me almost every day, even when she didn't call her mother.

Then one day, a year after she moved to New England, when I was into my 80's, I got a call from her that changed everything. She was almost yelling, and at first I thought something was wrong, that she had been injured or lost her job. When she finally settled down enough to speak coherently, she said, "I found her. I found your little girl on the beach." There followed a long silence. I had heard her words but they didn't compute. She might as well have been speaking Russian. "You found her?" I repeated dumbly. "How's that possible? She's not find-able."

"Yes, she is," she shouted, laughing and talking in such a jumble that I began to think she might be high on something. "She's looking for you!!" Another silence. Am I dreaming this?

How can any of this be true? Taking a deep breath, I said, "OK, Angela, I'm having trouble with this. Please start at the beginning and tell me slowly what the *hell* you're talking about."

"G-pa, listen to this. Your little girl on the beach is a grown woman now, and she remembers the time you gave her that feather. Apparently that meeting was as important to her as it was for you, and she's decided to try to find you. She launched a website and published the whole story on it – dates, details, everything. There can't be any doubt. It's her, and she wants to talk to you!"

I was too stunned to even think. She continued, "Mom can get it for you on the computer, and you can read it for yourself. And you can email her and tell her who you are and say that you want to find her, too." Pause. "She's been looking for you for over a year. She must really want to get in touch."

I thanked her and hung up. I had some serious work to do, emotional and mental. My angel was seven years old in a light blue bathing suit with a frilly skirt. What did all that have to do with some grown woman? Why would I want to see her? What would I have to say to her? Would talking to her destroy that precious memory? Wouldn't it be better to just leave things as they were?

But the family was having none of it. They were ecstatic about this miraculous development. My myth was about to take on flesh. "Aren't you curious?" they would ask. "Don't you want to know why she wants to find you?" Eventually, I agreed to let Ginger bring the letter up on her computer screen. She punched the key, the screen filled with a mass of information, Ginger smiled at me and got up from the chair. I sat down with very mixed feelings and began to read:

About twenty-four years ago, my mother and I spent a week

on the Outer Banks in N Carolina. I was seven years old at the time. On our first evening there, we were playing in the sand when a man came along and gave me a perfect white feather. He said something to me at the time, but left before I could learn anything about his identity. This encounter has been very significant for me in my adult years, and I would like to find this stranger to thank him for his gift, and to tell him why his thoughtful act to a little girl was so important.

Her name was Emily. That bit of information in itself, after all these years, was a shock. No longer Angel but now Emily. The site went on to add details about her later years, her family and her work. She was a physician's assistant in Virginia, was married, had a young son, and still loved the ocean. She was asking for people to assist in her quest. There was information about how to contact her, an indication of how long she had been conducting her search, as well as data on the astonishing number of people who had checked in to the site.

But I noticed immediately that her account of our meeting was missing several critical details. That was like a gong sounding in my ears – I was being invited to add the specific information which, out of all the people in the world, only I knew, information which would convince her that I was the person she was looking for. I suddenly visualized all the fakes who might have checked in claiming to be me, and I was gripped with a sense of outrage that others would try to steal my experience. At that moment I knew that I had to write her. I had no idea where all this would lead, but I felt that I had to see it through.

I had written only a few emails in my life, mostly to Angela, but, with Ginger's help, I sat down to compose my response to Emily, my demythologized Angel.

✝ ✝ ✝ ✝ ✝ ✝ ✝ ✝ ✝ ✝ ✝ ✝ ✝ ✝

III: Emily

I hadn't checked the site in almost two weeks. I got busy with other things, my son took a lot of my time, and by then I had just about given up on ever finding my feather-man, anyway. So when someone asked me if I had gotten any new responses and I said no, I realized that I didn't know. As a result, I logged on and started through the thirteen new emails on the feather site.

When I got down to the fifth one, I froze. There it was, the message I had been looking for for over a year, a response from the man who had been my unseen companion for most of my life. I read it through for a second time before I shouted to an empty house, "Here he is! I found him." He had written:

My granddaughter told me about your website on the web. She knew my story and recognized what you wrote. I am the man who gave you the feather back on the N Car beach that evening. I know you want the details. You were wearing a light blue bathing suit with a fluffy skirt, and you had strawberry blond hair. Your mother was working near the water and you were in the sand. You were both building a trench so the water could come up into the sand. The feather was white and about 6 in. long. That is all the detail I remember. Also, I said, Here, you need a feather.

I couldn't believe it! I had thought about this moment for years, had kidded myself about receiving an email from him, certain all the time that it would never happen. This was just a game, a way to play with my own personal myth, not a riddle to be solved.

But here it was, all of a sudden, the long-awaited answer to my childhood mystery. I was very confused. What if he was not a nice person? What if I was making a big fuss over something that meant nothing to him? Would talking to him ruin the image I had of this angelic presence who had once walked within an arm's length of me?

But it was too late now. The genie wouldn't fit back into the bottle, so I sat down and wrote him. He must have been using someone else's computer because I assumed that his name was not Ginger! But he didn't mention his own name. However, his recall of the details was startling, and the fact that he remembered them after all these years must indicate that the event had had some meaning for him, too. But how was that possible? He had walked by and disappeared in an instant. Why should he even remember doing that?

I told him more of my story, why his gift had meant so much to me over the years, and then asked for more details about himself. He responded promptly, and I found out that his name was Thomas and that he was a retired minister who was eighty-four years old. I was very glad I hadn't waited any longer to begin my quest, since we probably didn't have much time left. In later emails, he told me his story in greater detail, why he remembered giving me the feather, how he had idealized me and thought of me as his angel, in the same way I had come to think of him as my guardian and guide. It was at this point that I knew I had to go see him.

He lived in Maryland and I was still in southern Virginia, so I made an appointment and drove to his house one Saturday afternoon. I met his daughter, Ginger, who was waiting for me. But she had bad news. Thomas was in the hospital with what they were afraid was a stroke. She took me to the hospital and went into the room ahead of me. After preparing him for my visit, she came out said, "He's waiting for you."

I walked in cautiously, steeling myself for the first sight of him. He was propped up in bed, his arms lying on top of the blanket. He had a full head of snow white hair and his face was lined, but the lines only softened his expression and gave him a kindly appearance. He looked at me with glistening eyes as I leaned over and kissed him on the forehead. I sat in a chair by his bed and took hold of his warm hand.

We looked at each other in silence for a while, before he said, "Emily." It was almost as though he was testing the name, listening to the sound of it. "I always called you Angel."

"I know," I said. "I always thought of you as my angel, too." We sat looking into each other's eyes for a long time, sharing something deeper than words.

After a time, I said, "I've never forgotten you. I only saw you for a second but you have always been with me."

Tears were running down his cheeks now. He cleared his throat and said, "You were so beautiful, with the sun lighting up your hair. You've always been seven years old with a halo of pink fire."

More silence. Finally, I gently asked the question: "Why did you give me that feather?"

He started to answer several times before he could get the words out. "I thought you were an angel, and I figured you had shed it when you came to earth."

"Is that why you said, 'You need a feather'?" I asked him. He nodded.

I've forgotten the rest of our conversation because he kept nodding off. Once, when he seemed to rouse, I said, "I have something for you." He brightened for a moment, and I handed him the plastic sleeve in which I kept the white feather. "I want you to have this," I told him. "It belongs to both of us." I pulled it out of the sleeve and put it in his right hand; his other arm was not working properly. He looked at it intently, then looked at me, and there were twenty-four years of accumulated love in his expression.

I said, "You know, that feather saved my life many times. I don't think I would still be here if it wasn't for that feather." He smiled at me, another lovely, emotional smile.

I sat for a time and was thinking of leaving when he said quietly, "You know, I have loved you every day since I first saw you."

I couldn't stop the tears. I asked, "Why do you suppose all this happened?"

He was silent for a while and I thought he had drifted off again. Then he said, "Because we needed each other. Because that's how angels work. In disguise."

After a moment, I whispered, "I love you too, you know."

He didn't seem to hear. Then he roused himself and said with great intensity, "You gave me a wonderful gift. You gave me back my faith."

I was sobbing by this point. I hadn't done anything but pick up the feather that blew from his hand into mine. How could the simple act of receiving that gift result in such an enormous change in the giver? He gave me credit for something he had done for himself.

He finally slept, and Ginger came back in to retrieve me. Two weeks later she called to tell me he had died in his sleep. She was kind enough to say that my visit had made his passing easier for all of them.

IV: Thomas

I was anticipating the visit from Emily when, in the middle of the night, I woke up and couldn't move. Days in the hospital ensued and time lost all meaning. So it was a surprise when Ginger came in one afternoon to tell me that Emily was waiting outside to see me. I was frustrated to have to greet her in this condition, but I couldn't do anything about it. She came in and leaned over the bed to kiss me. I asked her to sit down so I could see her face.

"You know, I never got to see you," I reminded her. "All I saw was the top of your head and a little of your profile. I have to see if you're the same person and not an imposter." She looked at me full face, then slowly turned and offered me her profile. She was a pretty girl but her hair was blond. "You're a little bigger than I remember," I ventured.

She pretended to take offense. "That's not a polite thing to say to a lady."

I smiled. "Only in the vertical dimension," I assured her.

It is impolite to stare at another person, but this situation was so extraordinary that all rules were off. I apologized for examining her so closely, explaining, "I've been waiting for a quarter of a century to see what you look like. I wanted so badly to look at you, talk to you, spend some time with you, but I was afraid your mother would call the cops."

She nodded. "That kind of a situation is awkward," she agreed. After we had gazed at each other for a while, she asked, "Well, what do you think?"

I shook my head. "I got the best part of this deal," I said with a chuckle. "You're looking at a used-up old wreck, and I'm looking at the girl of my dreams."

"I've dreamt about you, too," she said. "Many times. You were always there, watching over me. When you gave me that feather, you gave me hope along with it." Her statement startled me, but I knew what she meant.

So I said, "Well, seeing you that day and watching you pick up the feather made it possible for me to hope again, too."

We looked at each other in astonishment. That tiny moment so long ago had had such enormous consequences in both our lives. After a while, she said, "I have a gift for you," and produced a blue plastic slip case with a transparent front. Inside was the feather.

"You kept it!" I said, somewhat surprised.

"Are you kidding?" she asked. "It's one of the main treasures of my life." She slid it out of the protective cover and put it in my good hand. I twirled it around, looking at it from every angle. It was bigger than I remembered, but just as white and with the same blue-gray stripe down the side. "I want you to have it," she said. "It really belongs to both of us."

I searched her face some more, simply overwhelmed by the visit. I had so much to say to her but couldn't think of a thing. "Your hair is supposed to be strawberry blond," I reminded her, shaking a finger.

"Sorry," she apologized, "but I've had to start coloring it."

"Well, you should be careful about that," I warned. "I might not have recognized you."

Soon, Ginger was escorting her out of the room and the visit was over. The woman was gone but the little girl on the beach was still there. After a while I got confused about who was who. Who was that woman who had come to see me and why was she bringing me a white feather? I had once given a similar feather to a little girl on the beach, and I have always remembered what beautiful curly hair she had, and how glorious it looked when it was backlit by the setting sun. But I've already told you that story, haven't I? I hate repeating myself.

28

V: Angela

I went to see G-pa the week before he died. My mother told me to get back home if I wanted to see him again, so I took the next plane. He looked feebler than the last time I had seen him, and it soon became obvious that he was getting confused.

I sat down by his bed and took his hand. He turned to me and smiled, a special intimate expression which I always thought he reserved for me. I asked him how the visit went. He leaned closer and said, "She was very nice, but I don't know where they got her."

I frowned and shook my head. "What do you mean? You know where we found her. On the Internet. She lives in Virginia."

He was silent for awhile. Almost to himself I could hear him say, "Nobody understands. She was a little girl."

I tried to help clear up his confusion. "But she's all grown up now."

He was struggling with it. "I didn't recognize her."

"Of course not," I said. "You wouldn't recognize her *because* she's all grown up."

But he persisted. "You don't understand. I gave the feather to a little girl. I wanted to see the little girl."

I reached into my purse and pulled out a photo that Emily had emailed to me. She apologized for not bringing it with her when she came for the visit. It was a picture taken by her mother during the week that they had spent at the Outer Banks. Emily was seven again, standing on the beach, holding a pail in one hand and a tiny beach shovel in the other. She was wearing the blue bathing suit with the frills, and her curly red hair glistened in the sun.

I handed it to G-pa and asked, "Is this the little girl you wanted to see?"

He took it in his good hand, stared at it for a very long time, and then I watched his face slowly crumple as the tears streamed down his cheeks.

"That's her," he said in a choked voice. "That's the little girl." He studied it some more. "I couldn't see her face before."

But his continuing confusion showed how much damage the stroke had done. "That woman who came was a blond. And she was a *woman!*" He held the photo out toward me. "This was the little girl I wanted to see again."

I decided to try to focus his thoughts on the girl rather than the woman. I asked him to repeat the story of the feather and the little girl, and he started the way he always had, but then got lost. I had never heard him forget the details before, and it scared me. I tried to calm him, but it was all becoming too much for him. He kept repeating, "She had strawberry blond hair." Then, as though seeing me for the first time, he said in surprise, "You do too. What's your name?"

I realized that we were losing the battle. "I'm Angela, Honey. I'm your granddaughter." I started to cry because I no longer knew what to say. He rambled on for awhile, mumbling about the woman who had come to see him.

I finally realized that, for him, Emily would always be the little girl in the blue bathing suit. That reality had nothing to do with a real person who grew up and changed. In his mind, she was a changeless, eternal little innocent, holding his feather and transforming his life with her mystic presence. He could not reconcile the real person with the myth.

I went back the next day, but he was past talking. He lay with his head on the pillow, looking at me with a shadow of recognition, smiling at what I said, but no longer able to respond. His right hand was curled up onto his chest, and in that hand he held the photo of his Angel. The feather lay on the bed alongside him.

He died a couple of days later. Emily was invited to the funeral but said it would be too painful. She didn't go into detail but I knew what she was feeling. Her myth revolved around a tall, healthy stranger who could walk and speak, not a wasted old body lying in a casket. The effort to find him had been a success, but the reality could never begin to displace the myth. Yet, without the search, he would never have been able to see the photo of his little red-headed girl in those last days of his life. That picture became the final treasure of his 84 years.

I spoke at the funeral. I told the story one last time and marveled with the mourners how one tiny act of kindness had been able to transform two lives and affect dozens of others. G-pa had spent more than two decades mining the riches of love and faith that followed from that chance encounter. He had shown all of us the abiding value that can be found in the tiniest events of life.

II

Memories

When Sean Milling was about nine, his parents enrolled him in a class for children at a local swim club, and he quickly showed signs that he might have the potential to become a competitive swimmer. Some of his friends were in the class and they loved taking the lessons together. But the best part of the session came at the end. The instructors paired those who were qualified and had them race each other across the width of the pool. Those who lost were eliminated, and the pairings continued in tourney form until one person was declared the winner for that night.

There were about forty kids in the class, of whom half were competent to take part in the races. It was the final event of each swim session, and the boys all talked about it eagerly, boasting about who they were going to beat this time. On the night of the third class session, Sean won. And he won almost every night after that for the remainder of the year. The coaches were soon making greater plans for him, and the other boys were gunning for his title and reputation.

The notoriety was an important factor in Sean's life. He was a little shorter than the rest of the boys going into fifth grade and, although he was a good student, he had a tendency to, shall we say, embellish the truth about himself to compensate for his short stature. He was so good at bragging about his exploits, however, that his friends swallowed at least

33

half of his stories. And he had become skilled at producing evidence to prove his claims, so that the boys who admired him eagerly shared his stories with each other. In short, he already had a reputation for superior skills, so that his successes in the pool seemed to confirm the rest of his claims.

One of those claims involved a boy's camp in upper New York State which he had attended the previous summer. Although it was a regular summer camp, he let it be known that it had been a sort of farm team training camp for young boys who one day hoped to play for the New York Yankees. When he told his friends that he had been named MVP for the summer, they didn't believe him. But then he brought to school a very impressive plaque, claiming to have been awarded it at the end of the summer. It had his name, Sean Milling, prominently displayed above the legend, "Most Valuable Player, New York Yankees Youth Training Camp, 1989," and it was apparently signed by Dallas Green, Yankees' General Manager. What he failed to tell his friends was that he had paid to have the plaque made, using money he earned on his paper route.

At the end of the school year, in the summer of 1990 when Sean was almost ten years old, his family took one of their rare vacations. Someone had loaned them the use of a cottage on Silver Lake in the Adirondacks, and they drove there on a Saturday afternoon, planning to enjoy a week of swimming, boating and outdoor fun. It was a beautiful location with wide sandy beaches and low, pine-covered mountains. As soon as they got settled in the cottage, Sam, Sean's father, suggested that they go for their first swim. He said, "Sean, you're going to love swimming in the lake. It's a whole different experience from the pool at the swim club."

Sean had never been to a lake before, and was already wondering how far he could swim in open water. He also wondered if they could organize some competitive events between the other vacationers along the shore.

Sean and his older sister, Anita, changed into their bathing suits and walked down to the beach. He called to his father, "Hurry up. I want to swim with you." His mother, standing on the front porch of the cottage, gave a derisive laugh. Sean heard her say, "That'll be the day!"

He frowned and took a few steps toward her. "Isn't Daddy coming?"

His father came out onto the porch just as his mother said with amusement, "Your father can't swim. He's afraid of the water!"

Sean was shocked. Could this be possible? His father, putting one arm around his wife's back to quiet her, called out, "You go on and have fun with Anita. I'll watch you from here." Bewildered, Sean turned and started for the water. He had never known this about his father, and wondered why he would come to the lake if he was afraid of the water.

Anita had run ahead and was splashing in the clear water, screaming when she realized how cold it was. But, as Sean approached the water's edge, something came over him. It was as though someone had poured lead into his head and it rapidly filled his body, building in weight and pressure until it burst out the top of his head. It was dread. He had never before experienced dread, and it paralyzed him.

His legs turned to rubber and he collapsed on the sand a foot from the edge of the lake. His father, watching Anita jumping about in joy, at first was unaware of what had happened to Sean. When he saw him sitting huddled on the beach, he called, "Go on in, Sean. The water's fine! I want to see you swim in it."

When Sean didn't move, Sam stepped down off the porch, walked towards the lake and reached out a hand to grab Sean's shoulder. At that point, the boy burst into terrified screams, crying hysterically and digging his fingers into the sand as though to anchor himself so he couldn't be moved.

Sam, shocked by this unexpected behavior, knelt by him and asked what was wrong. Sean's chest hurt so much from the racking sobs that he could hardly breathe, much less talk. His father kept pressing him for an explanation, demanding that he calm down, but there was no reasoning with him. Sean was so hysterical that he couldn't even walk, which meant that his father had to pick him up and carry him back to the cottage where he spent the rest of the afternoon in bed.

That night he had the dream for the first time.

It was the vividness of the dream that got his attention, perhaps because he had nothing to compare it with. He seemed to be an observer watching the action take place, while at the same time looking out through the eyes of the young boy.

The symbolism was so clear that the dream seemed to be demanding that he recognize the setting. He wore a workman's cap with a bill, a long black woolen coat and wooden clogs, and in the background was a windmill surrounded by masses of tulips. He realized instantly that he was a young Dutch boy.

In the dream, he was walking along a road which ran by a lake, carrying a large basket made of woven reeds. In the basket was a dead, plucked goose, its head hanging over the basket's edge and swinging with every step. The boy looked to be about Sean's age, ten or slightly older, and he was whistling as he went.

Through the odd intuitive knowledge by which dreams provide their own captions, he knew that he had just spent a major part of the family's meager funds on the goose, which was to be the main course for a special 70th birthday dinner celebration for his grandfather.

Sean, or rather, the Dutch boy, had been chosen to run this

important errand since everyone else was busy either working or preparing dinner, and he was the only one who could be spared. His mother had grabbed him by the coat collar as he left, and had sternly reminded him of the importance of his mission. Without the goose, his family would not eat, and the money with which he was being entrusted was a small fortune to a family which had almost nothing. He had promised to be careful.

As he walked along the road, which was separated from the edge of the lake by only a few feet, three teenage boys on bicycles came along from behind him. They passed him single file, and the first one grabbed the cap off Sean's head and threw it into the water. As he turned to see where his cap had landed, one of the other boys put his foot in the middle of Sean's back and gave him a shove, so that he went flying. His arms flailed out in front of him, the basket launched itself out of his hands, and both basket and goose landed in the water.

Crying out in alarm, he dropped to his belly and peered over the edge of the embankment. The water was covered with an interwoven mass of the large green leaves of water plants, and the basket lay on top of them, upside down and partly submerged. He could just reach it over the foot-high drop-off to the water's surface. But when he retrieved the basket, the goose was gone.

Horrified, he leaned back over the edge and tried to reach down into the water through the tough, scratchy leaves. Not being able to reach the bottom from that position, he sat up and, without taking off his clogs, stuck his feet into the water to try to locate the bird. However, because he had removed the basket, he had no clear idea where the goose might have fallen. Finally, with increasing alarm, he jumped down into the water and felt around with his hands. Success! He found the bird, grabbed it by its slimy neck, and threw it up on the bank. But when he turned to climb out of the water, the muck on the bottom of the lake sucked off his clogs, leaving him barefoot.

Since he had no desire to walk home along the stony road without clogs, and knowing that he would be soundly thrashed if he told his father he had lost his shoes, he reached back down into the water hoping to find them quickly. However, while the fat goose had been easy to locate, his clogs were stuck in deep muck at the bottom of the lake, and his arms were too short to reach that far.

Since all Dutch boys knew how to swim, he had no problem ducking under the surface. He took a deep breath and went down on his hands and knees between the tangle of stems and leaves that crowded the water. He felt around in the soft muck but found nothing. Widening the area of his search, he unwittingly moved out into deeper water. When he tried to stand up to take another breath, a number of things – disorientation, his water-logged overcoat, the tangle of plant stems trapping his arms, his inability to find a firm footing – all combined to defeat him. In his struggles, he sucked in a lungful of water, panicked, and was instantly free of the water.

Except that now he was *above* the water! He was looking down on the riverbank where he could see his basket and the goose lying in a grotesque position. But he himself was nowhere to be seen.

The dream scared Sean so badly that he woke up gasping for breath. His crying attracted his mother who did her best to soothe him. "There, there, you just had a bad dream. Now think of something nice, and lie down and go back to sleep."

But the images kept swimming through his head, and they almost succeeded in recreating the dread that he had felt earlier that day when he had tried to go swimming. He finally fell back to sleep, and the next morning forgot about the experience. It was a Sunday so they all went to church and, because of the strict Sabbatarian beliefs of his parents, they were not allowed to go swimming. So he was spared having to deal with that strange fear of the water which he had so unexpectedly experienced the day before.

They walked partway around the lake and later sat on the beach, enjoying the June weather. Anita and he built sand castles and dug holes at the shoreline, read and played board games in the cottage. Television was another thing not permitted on Sundays.

That night he went to bed as usual, tired, sleepy, and without any particular worries. But again at about two a.m., he had the same dream in even more vivid detail. He seemed to know what was going to happen when the boys came along on their bicycles, but he was powerless to move out of their way. As he plunged into the water looking for his clogs, the water plants became like a rope mesh, grasping him, binding his hands, trussing him up like his dead goose. He felt the searing pain in his chest as his body screamed for air, and the suffocating sensation of water entering his mouth and lungs.

And then he was above the lake once again, free, calm, without pain or anxiety. He looked down on the basket and goose lying on the bank, and felt oddly detached from them. In one corner of his mind, the thought lingered for a moment – "My mother is going to be disappointed when I don't bring the goose home." But that part of his life seemed far away and unimportant, almost as though the people were part of someone else's family. And then he was awake.

He couldn't decide how to react. The end of the dream had actually had a calming effect on him, but then he remembered the feeling of smothering, causing the frightening sensations to return with a jolt. He started to cry loudly, and his mother hurried in for a second time, a little less patient than the night before. He said, "I had the same dream and it felt like I was drowning again."

She sat on the bed, smoothed his hair and said, "Well, it was only a dream. It can't hurt you. It's all in your head." Then getting a little more serious, she added, "I don't know why you dream about being afraid of the water. You're a wonderful swimmer. You're not going to drown. If you fell into the water, you'd know what to do." She waited a moment. "Isn't that right?"

He nodded reluctantly. "But," he protested, "why do I dream about drowning if I can swim? And why am I a Dutch boy?"

"I don't know, dear," she said. "Dreams are funny things. Go back to sleep, and have pleasant dreams for a change."

As she left, he asked her, "Why is Daddy afraid of the water?"

She turned with an impatient look on her face, and said, "I don't know. He always has been."

"You don't make him go in the lake."

"You're not like him, Sean. That's why I sent you to take swimming lessons. I don't want you to be afraid of the water like he is. Now go to sleep and don't worry about these things."

The next day, they rented a small motorboat in the morning and drove all around Silver Lake. They stopped for lunch at a little café on a pier where they ate foot-long hotdogs, the first ones Sean had ever seen. There was a small playground at another spot across the lake, and their parents paid the fee so that Anita and he could play on the equipment. The main attraction was a child's roller coaster, tiny cars that accommodated two people and traveled on tubular steel rails up and down slight inclines. Anita rode in back, her arms protectively around her brother, and they liked it so much that they rode it three times.

They got back to the cottage after two o'clock, and Sam announced that it was time to go swimming. Sean put on his swimsuit with some misgivings, but was determined to go in the water this time. However, as he got to the water's edge, it happened again. It was like he hit a brick wall. He was powerless to go any farther. It was as though he had lost control of his body. He could not take that final step into the water.

Sam came down from the cottage and said, with some displeasure, "Sean, don't do this again. We're here at the lake to have a nice week and do some swimming. You're a good swimmer. Why are you refusing to go in?"

Sean was disgusted with himself, frightened at this strange feeling, and upset at his father's insistence. "How come it's OK for you to be afraid of the water, and not me?"

His father was silent for a moment, then said, "I don't know why I'm afraid. I have been all my life. I've missed a lot of fun because I couldn't go in the water. I don't want you to be like me. And you're not. You're a good swimmer. I'm very proud of you. So why not just go in and have fun?"

Sean thought for a while. "How do you feel when you try to go in the water?"

Sam looked at him, trying to collect his thoughts, and said, "My knees get weak, my stomach wants to throw up, and I feel like I'm going to faint."

"That's just how I feel," said Sean angrily. "Why do you force me to go in when you don't have to do it yourself?"

Sam sat down alongside of Sean. "You're right. I don't know why you're afraid of the lake, but at least you can swim at the club. Maybe it has something to do with the size of the lake."

All Sean could say was, "I can't help it." He sat on the beach in a miserable funk and dug angry holes in the sand, watching a dozen people from the area having a good time romping in the water.

When they got back to the cottage, everybody was upset with him, especially Anita who complained, "I don't have anybody to swim with." He tried to make it clear that he couldn't help himself, that his body wouldn't let him go in, but his mother wouldn't tolerate such nonsense. "You'll just have to try harder. I won't have this defiant attitude!"

Well, it was one thing for her to tell him to behave differently, and quite another for him to tell his body to behave differently. But she made him promise to try. He went to bed not thinking about dreaming but about how he could overcome his nervous reaction, or whatever it was, and get into the water tomorrow.

However, around two o'clock the dream returned. For the third time, the sensation of drowning got more intense and crushing, while the experience of floating at the end was so powerful and almost joyful that it erased the trauma of his death and left him at peace. He woke up but this time didn't feel the need to call his mother. Yet, he desperately wanted the dreams to stop, even though something told him that they held an important message for him.

When he told his mother about it in the morning, she dismissed the dream as well as his concern about it.

"We all dream," she said.

"But we don't all die every night. It scares me."

She thought for a moment. "Well, you need to stop worrying about it. You're not going to drown, and obsessing about it just makes it keep happening."

On Tuesday, he forced himself to put his feet in the water while his butt was still on the sand. That was a big step, but his feet felt like they were burning and he didn't keep them in very long. Other than those mandated swimming periods, he enjoyed the week, except for the fact that the dream recurred every night. The family went boating, took in movies, drove through the mountains to sightsee, and continued their walks around the lake, alternating directions every day. But toward the end of the week, those family walks began to take on a strange kind of urgency for Sean. He begged his father to go with him every day and to walk farther each time. It was as if something was pulling him around the lake, some goal, some destination which he didn't understand. It felt as though there was something that needed to be discovered.

On Friday afternoon, he found out what it was.

They woke up on Friday, the last day of their vacation, to discover that it was pouring rain. That shattered their plans for a picnic on the island in the middle of the lake. It also cut out boating, taking another of their walks, and cancelled their final trip to the kiddie park. But in addition, it made swimming out of the question! Sean was secretly glad he didn't have to spend another day listening to their demands that he go into the water.

However, there was still that insistent urging from somewhere inside him to complete their hike around the lake. They had gone partway in either direction, but the opposite end of the lake remained unexplored. They had seen it at a distance from lakeside, but Sean had a restless desire, almost a gut need, to walk the trail on the back side of the lake.

He was going to start begging his father to drive them over there when, to his astonishment, his father suggested the very thing. "Since we can't play outdoors today," he said, "why don't we do a little more exploring in the car? Sean has been begging to see the other end of the lake, as though there is some buried treasure there waiting for him." They all agreed, so they loaded up the car after lunch and took off.

It was their intention, if the weather didn't moderate, to take in another movie after their jaunt around the lake. His mother was hopeful, however, that the rain would stop, in which case she wanted to drive up in the mountains to a well-known scenic overlook. So they set out full of anticipation.

The lake was only about ten miles in circumference so it didn't take long to drive around it. But as they followed the curving shoreline, Sean began to feel the same kind of panic building that he had experienced on their first day. This time it was accompanied by a muffled roaring in his ears, which made it increasingly difficult to hear what was being said in the car.

They were driving clockwise around lake, and he was sitting on the right side of the car looking out the window. The panicky sensation and the noise in his ears served to narrow his field of vision, so that all he could see was the water flashing past, partially obscured by the trees that crowded the shoreline. As they approached the back side of the lake, the area which had been silently pulling him toward it for the past two or three days, he started to have trouble breathing. It was as though an invisible hand had been placed over his mouth and he had to breathe through his nose. As he struggled for breath, the panic turned to a burning pressure in his chest, and he was about to cry out for help.

But at that moment he saw the rock.

It was a huge boulder, perched on a high slope above the edge of the lake, just to the right of a dense stand of trees. At that instant, the roaring ended and there was total silence in his head.

"Stop!" he shouted to his father. "Stop the car!"

His vision was riveted to that large rock and, as he stared at it. another layer was added to what he was looking at, as though someone had slipped a transparent slide over the scene. Two people were moving alongside the boulder, carrying what looked like a body. Suddenly, Sean knew what was happening, remembered seeing it happen; it was happening to *him*!

He jumped out into the drizzle and started to run toward the boulder. But his mother was out of the car an instant later, demanding in a stern voice that he stop. He turned to look at her. "This is where it happened," he shouted. "I know what happened here."

His father was standing by the driver's door, telling him to get back in the car. Sean walked around behind the car and said to his father, "You have to let me go down there. I have to see it." Then he added, "Come with me!"

"Go down where?" his father asked in a bewildered tone.

"To the water," Sean said impatiently. "I have to see something."

"What is there to see? It's all muddy down there."

"I have to see if it's there, if the pipe is there," he shouted. He was getting more frustrated by the moment.

"What pipe?" His father was totally confused by Sean's behavior and was beginning to lose patience.

"The pipe where it happened, where they put me," he said, stamping his foot in exasperation.

"Where what happened? Will you please make sense?"

"Where I *died*!" he shouted

Silence. His mother had come around and the three of them stood by the open car door, the shock of that statement echoing between them.

"What did you say?" his father started to ask. But his wife cut him off.

"What nonsense," she said in a huff. "Get back in the car. You're getting soaked."

He turned pleading eyes to his father. "Please come with me. I have to see it. I'll go by myself!"

Sam stared at Sean for a moment, then sighed, told his wife to wait in the car, and followed Sean who had started to run toward the large rock. Sean shouted over his shoulder, "When

45

you see the pipe, you'll know I'm telling the truth."

There was a path to the right side of the boulder winding its way down to the water's edge. Sean stumbled along it, frantic with excitement and fear, but knowing that something important was happening. When he got to the water's edge, he turned left onto another trail that ran parallel to the water. Fifteen feet further along, he came to a little stream flowing down the hill and emptying into the lake. Heedless of the fact that he was standing in the stream, he turned to look back up the hill. And there it was.

His father caught up with him and, finally out of patience, told him to get out of the water. But Sean just pointed up the hill. Sam looked in the direction that Sean was indicating, and saw the opening of a large metal drainage culvert, four feet in diameter.

"See!" Sean shouted triumphantly. "I told you it was here."

His father shook his head, mystified. "So there's a pipe here. What difference does that make?

All the boy could do was smile. Oblivious to his father's irritation, he asked, "Don't you want to know how I knew it was here?"

"You saw it from the lake," Sam said, throwing up his hands.

"No," he said, excited to be able to put the thought into words. "This is where they put me before I drowned."

"*What*? What on earth are you talking about?"

"But back then," he added, "I was a woman!"

From the moment Sean left the car, the whole scenario was playing in his mind, its details as sharp as any TV program. But he needed to rewind it and watch it from the beginning, just to check his memory of the event. It was as though he had always known what had happened here long ago, but it had been covered up. The sight of the boulder seemed to knock that cover loose, and it simply slid off and exposed the truth.

He walked up near the pipe, ignoring his father who was demanding that he quit his irrational behavior and get out of the water. Several feet from the opening, Sean turned and faced the lake. What he really wanted to do was to climb into the pipe, but he realized that his father would drag him bodily back up the hill if he tried something like that.

With his back to the metal culvert and his feet in the short stream rushing down from the drainage pipe into the lake six feet away, he stopped for a moment and closed his eyes. Pushing some kind of mental switch, he let the memory roll.

His name was Mildred and it was late at night because the only light came from the moon. He was in terrible pain and kept fainting. His hands were tied behind him and there was tape over his mouth. Two men were carrying him, and he recalled seeing that boulder as they struggled past it down toward the lake. They shoved him into the drainage pipe feet-first and left. Then he was in the water and he couldn't breath. At that point the mental replay ended, and the scene seemed to blend into that dark night from somewhere in his past.

As he came back to the present, he heard his father yelling at him, demanding that he come back to the car. Sean hurried to join him because he had learned what he needed to know.

His mother threw a fit when he got in the car alongside Anita. "What were you thinking, young man! You're soaking wet; now we'll have to go back to the cottage and get you changed. I hope you're happy that you've ruined the last day of our vacation."

Then, fixing him with her eyes, she asked, "What on earth caused you to jump out of the car that way? I'm beginning to get worried about your erratic behavior!"

She was waiting for an answer, but he knew how she was going to react. He tried to defuse the tension: "There was something down there I had to see."

His mother started to say something, but his father broke in. "He ran down there to see the open end of an iron culvert."

"But I knew it was there," Sean protested.

His mother was shaking her head. "If you already knew it was there, why did you have to go see it? And how did you know it was there? And," she said, her tone getting harsher, "what does a drainage pipe have to do with you, anyway?"

When he didn't respond, she turned back around and said to his father, "I guess he'll have to spend the rest of the day in his room. This is an awful way to end our vacation."

They had arrived at the cottage by this time, and his parents made him take a shower and put on his bedclothes. They left him alone in his bedroom for an hour or so, which gave his mother a chance to calm down. She came into his room late in the afternoon in a slightly more reasonable mood. Sitting on his bed, she looked at him with concern and said, "Your father has been telling me some of the things you said to him. I want you to repeat them to me."

"What part?"

"The part where you told him what you think happened there."

"You won't believe me," he said defensively.

"It's not about my believing you. It's about finding out what *you* believe."

Sean thought for a long time about how to say the right thing. "Will you just let me tell you what I saw? And not tell me I'm crazy or lying?"

"Yes," she said quietly. "I will do that."

He took a deep breath. "I know that I drowned there. Bad men put me in that pipe and I landed in the lake and drowned."

His mother, trying to be patient, said, "Why don't you start at the beginning and tell me the whole story as you think it happened."

Sean searched her eyes for a moment and then began. He said he saw himself walking up a dirt road which led to an old filling station above which was a sign that read "Evans Gas and Oil." Sean described the appearance of the place as he walked through the large overhead garage door, then turned right and went into the office area. Taking a deep breath, he told her his memory in the present tense, as though it was happening just then.

Sean/Mildred is behind the counter at one end of the office. S/he understands that she is the daughter of the owner, that her name is Mildred Evans, and that she is about thirty years old. It is late at night, she's alone and in the process of closing up. Two men come in and start asking questions, but she tries to get rid of them. She sees their car outside and thinks it's odd that they have left the motor running even though the car is empty. It's an old car like those in the 1930's.

One of the men pulls a gun and demands money. She reaches into the register for the shop's pistol, but he sees her do it and shoots her in the right shoulder. She falls on the floor as the other guy hops over the counter and cleans out the register. Then they grab her and throw her in the backseat of the car and drive off.

Her hands are tied behind her and they have put tape over her mouth. They carry her past a large boulder and down toward a lake. There they shove her into a drainage pipe feet-first and leave. She lies there for a long time until she hears it start to rain. It is a terrible downpour and she is relieved at first that they have not left her out in the open.

But then the water starts rushing down the drain pipe. As it gets deeper, the flow picks up speed and power and eventually flushes her out into the lake. The force of the discharge dumps her about ten feet out into the water, where it is four or five feet deep. She struggles to stand, but her ankles are tied together, and in the pitch dark she isn't sure where the shore is and she keeps falling, totally disoriented. The tape is forcing her to breathe through her nose, but every time she falls she gets more water up her nose. She can't spit it out and begins to panic.

And then the vision ended and the screen of Sean's mind went black, as if someone had turned off the television.

His mother looked at him awhile, started to speak several times, then finally asked slowly, "And why do you want to tell us this story?"

"Because it's true," he said deliberately, "because I saw it all happen."

She nodded slightly. "And who did you say you were when all this is supposed to have happened?"

He knew he had lost any hope of convincing her. But she kept prodding and he finally said, "A lady. Her name was Mildred."

She smiled a kind of superior parental smile, and said, "Do you know how crazy this sounds, Sean? What would you think if I told you a story like that?"

"I would believe you," he shot back, "if you told me it was true."

"Well," she said, muttering half to herself, "I don't know what to do about this imagination of yours. Maybe I'll have to take you to the doctor." Then she stood up and left the room.

The following morning after breakfast, when his parents were packing, Sean appeared in the living room in his bathing suit. His mother gave him an exasperated look. "Get your clothes on, Sean. We're ready to leave. What do you think you're doing anyway?"

"I'm going swimming," he shouted as he ran out the front door. He jumped into the water, swam out twenty yards, then turned to see the three of them standing on the porch, their mouths open in disbelief.

Sean's mother made an appointment for him to talk with a friend of the family, Dr. Fielding, who happened to be a psychologist. They met in his home one evening soon after. When they had filled the doctor in on some of the background story, he looked at Sean and in a friendly voice asked, "Why were you willing to swim on Saturday when you were so scared to do it all week?"

Sean wasn't sure how to explain it. "After I saw the pipe and remembered drowning, I knew why I was afraid. And I wasn't afraid anymore." Then he added, "I knew I wasn't going to drown now because I had already drowned a long time ago."

Dr. Fielding asked Sean to tell him the whole story in his own words. Sean repeated as many of the details as he could remember, while the doctor sat looking him in the eye and nodding. He sensed a sincerity in Sean that made his story seem less of a fabrication.

When Sean had finished, Dr. Fielding told him to stand up and take his shirt off. Sean thought it was an odd request but he complied. The doctor called him closer and put his hands on both of the boy's shoulders. Then he leaned forward and peered closely at the area just below Sean's right shoulder.

"How long have you had this dark spot?" he asked. Sean looked down, trying to see what he was talking about. There, five inches below the top of his shoulder, Sean could see a round spot on his skin, faint but unmistakable, the diameter of a large pencil and maroon in color.

"That's always been there," Sean told him. "Why? What does it mean?"

Dr. Fielding didn't answer. "Turn around," he said with a motion of his head. A moment later Sean heard him whisper,

"My god!"

"What?!" Sean asked, feeling a little scared.

The doctor took him over to a big mirror on the back of the hall door, holding up a hand mirror so Sean could see something on his own back. The doctor pointed it out, a somewhat darker spot, also maroon, but more jagged and about an inch across. It was directly opposite the spot on the front of Sean's shoulder.

Sean still didn't get the significance of all this. Dr. Fielding went back to his chair and thought for a moment. When Sean pressed him for an explanation, the doctor said, "Tell me the part of the story where you got the gun out of the register. What happened next?"

"The man saw me," he said, "and he shot me before I could shoot him."

"Where did he shoot you?" the doctor asked quietly.

"Right here," the boy said, pointing to his right shoulder. But when he looked down, he saw that his finger was resting right on top of the birthmark. Their eyes locked and Sean froze.

"What...how...?" he stuttered.

After a moment, the doctor said, "Well, if you had been shot in this lifetime, I would say that those were the scars of the bullet wound." He wiggled his finger for Sean to come closer. "This," he said, pointing to the mark on his shoulder, "looks like an entrance wound. And the mark on your back is clearly an exit wound."

There was a stunned silence in the room. After a moment, the doctor said, "I've read about this phenomenon but I've never seen an example before. It's called a psychic scar, a birthmark which is supposed to be the body's memory of an injury that occurred in a previous life, often the wound that caused the person's death."

Sean plopped down on his chair, stunned. Then he let out a

loud whoop and started to laugh excitedly. "This proves it. Now you know I'm not lying."

"Well now, Sean," the doctor said, trying to calm him down, "by itself this doesn't prove anything. We'd need more information."

"Like what?" Sean demanded. He was ready to do anything to make his case. But the doctor had resources that Sean knew nothing about. He contacted certain friends of his and had them do some research.

A week later, he stopped by the house one evening and pulled a letter from his pocket. With an amused smile, he told them that he had something to read to them. He unfolded the piece of paper and began:

"Lake County police today arrested two men who have been charged in the Silver Lake murder which occurred a month ago. In a written statement, one of the suspects confessed to placing the victim in a rainwater discharge pipe from which she was probably flushed into the lake by the force of the outflow. The victim was bound and gagged, and was thus unable to save herself."

He looked at them, raising his eyebrows in amazement. "Do you want to hear the victim's name?" Everyone nodded warily. "Her name was...Mildred Evans and she was thirty-two years old. And this newspaper article is dated...June 19, 1933."

III

The Key

When I was a kid, just after World War II, I knew all the makes and models of cars. It was a lot simpler back then; each make of car had a sedan, a coupe, a convertible and a wagon. And that was it. You could tell a Chevrolet from a Pontiac from an Oldsmobile from a Buick from a Cadillac, even though they were all made by General Motors. This relatively simpler situation reflected the simpler times in which we were living, right after the end of the biggest war in history.

When I was a teen ager, I used to take photos of all the new models as they came out in September, and put them in a big scrapbook. Even when I was twenty, it was exciting to see how the 1950 models were going to look different from the 1949's. Up through 1949, most of the new cars were remakes of the prewar models. Everyone was so desperate for a new car after the war that the manufacturers didn't have to think about innovations. They just cranked out the old models, and they couldn't keep them on the showroom floor. There was often a three-month waiting period for a new car, so you didn't care if it was more modern than the last model. All you wanted to do was to get the thing in your garage as quickly as possible. That ended in 1950 when the first truly postwar models began to come off the assembly lines.

The 1942 models were the last pre-war cars to be made; after that, the war effort snapped up all the manufacturing facilities, and they stopped making cars for civilian use. The 1942 Chevrolet had a model called the Fleetline Aerosedan. It was a fastback with a sloping rear deck that looked streamlined. This model was often painted in two-tone colors with, for instance, a chocolate top and a tan bottom below the beltline. It was a beautiful car for that time, and the classiest thing you could own. The problem was that they were only built from September 1941 to February 1942. After that, you just plain couldn't get one. I lusted after that car, but I was only thirteen in 1942 so my love affair was a hopeless one.

I was born in October 1929, the month when the stock market collapsed. So when 1979 rolled around and I turned fifty, I experienced another kind of collapse. It hit me as a profound shock that here I was, more than halfway through my life, starting to slide down the backside of my years, and what had I accomplished? Nothing. Death was coming closer every minute and I had nothing to leave my family. My job as a metal shop instructor at the local Vo-Tech school was dead end and, though I enjoyed the kids, I didn't make enough to take care of my own kids as I had planned. I loved my family, but the stress of always being short of money took the edge off of my pleasure in life. Instead of being ahead of the curve, I was always running to catch up. The more I tried to moonlight, the less time I had with my kids. I just couldn't seem to work out a winning strategy.

My unbelievably generous and thoughtful wife, Audrey, knew all this, of course, and was looking around for some special way in which to make her husband forget that he was now a half-century old. [She was only forty-three at the time!] So she did what most men would never believe a wife capable of doing – she shoved a copy of Hemmings in front of my five-decade-old eyes. If you're not familiar with Hemmings, it is to the antique car collector what the Bible is to a Presbyterian. It is *the* magazine for old car enthusiasts.

Audrey apologized for coming up with a birthday gift which was no longer a surprise, but she said, "I didn't want to do this without your knowledge and agreement." She was smart about that because of our cash flow. Even with my salary and spare jobs, we barely got through the months. Audrey could have worked – she was a nurse's aide – but we decided she should stay at home with our four children, a job which was even more fulltime than mine! We were married in 1956 and the kids were born in 1958, 1960, 1963 and 1968, which made them 21, 19, 16 and 11 in 1979. They were all still at home including Joe, Jr., the eldest, who was a welder. Jessica, the oldest girl, attended a junior college in town and lived at home, too. Annabelle and Raymond were in high school and elementary school, respectively.

What Audrey was rubbing under my nose was a photo of a 1942 Chevrolet Fleetline Aerosedan! As I looked at it, my heart leapt within my bosom, as they say, and I had a sensation similar to what I felt when I first laid eyes on Audrey. It wasn't beautiful, but it-was-beautiful!!!, if you know what I mean. It was a bit pitted with rust, was all one solid dark color, and was missing some glass. Other than that, it appeared to be intact. It was currently in Pittsburgh, an hour away, and the owner wanted $300 for it.

I looked at my wife and she looked at me and together we looked at the photo. She leaned over and whispered in my ear, "I thought that would make a nice 50th birthday present. Now that you're over the hill, I don't want you to buy a Triumph and start chasing women. This looks to be more your style and speed."

She knew her man. I was on the phone so fast that I left skid marks on the magazine. The man said the car was still there and was drivable. I told him we would take it, and that we would be down to get it on the weekend. My birthday wasn't for another month, but I wasn't taking any chances. Joey immediately offered to help restore it, as I knew he would, and we were impatient to get our hands on the thing.

Audrey stole $100 out of her house money jar, I added $100 which I had been planning to use for a birthday present for myself, a new fly rod, and Joey, bless his heart, threw in the other $100. So on Saturday we packed five of us (Jessica had classes to attend) into my old 1969 Buick SportWagon, and made our way down to Pittsburgh.

The Hemmings photo was obviously an old one, because the car was in worse shape than I was prepared for. Its upholstery was shot, the engine clearly needed an overhaul, and the shocks were...shocking. I pointed these things out to the old man who was trying to unload it on us, and talked him down another $50. He was a funny little old fellow with curly white hair and a French accent. His name was Herbert Marchand. We handed him the cash and shook hands.

I cranked her up and Joey followed me in the station wagon. The two kids rode in the backseat of the '42, complaining all the way home about the smell and the condition of the cushions. It didn't take me long to realize that my new pride and joy didn't have any brakes. I told Joey, at one stop, to be prepared to catch me with his car bumper if I started to coast backward on a hill somewhere. I could hold it on the hills only by slipping the clutch, but apparently the old guy had already been doing that for years since the clutch was all but inoperable.

It took us two hours to cover the fifty miles home, where I put my birthday present in the old barn we used for storage. Joey and I went out after dark and stood looking at it for a full minute. Then we looked at each other and burst into giddy laughter. "What were we thinking?" we asked in unison.

However, the car had promise, it *was* an Aerosedan, something I had wanted my whole life, and we were anxious to get to it. Joey was even more excited about the project than I was, and was a tremendous help. His ideas and skill were exactly what I needed.

We worked on it in our spare time, and it was fun cooperating on the project. We disassembled the body, removed the doors and the hatch, put it on blocks to remove the wheels, and stripped the inside so it was totally empty.

That was when I discovered the key.

I was tearing the mat out of the hatch compartment behind the rear seat when the ragged material under the mat caught on something. When I got the mat loose, I saw what looked like the pointed end of a key sticking out of an overlapping joint in the metal floor. I had to get a screwdriver to pry it loose, ripping open a finger in the process. When I finally got it out, it proved to be a safety deposit key. It had the number 4037 on it but no indication of which bank it belonged to.

I put it on my dresser while we continued to work on the car. But it nagged at me – whose was it, where was the safety deposit box, what was in that box? The reason I didn't move immediately on my curiosity, however, was because of a moral question – who did the key belong to, me or the former owner of the car? I couldn't just ignore that issue.

One day, I decided to get serious about the quest. I called the old man who had sold me the car, but got an intercept which stated that the number was out of service. Thinking that I could either return the key to him or learn what bank it belonged to, I drove back down to his place the next weekend. He wasn't there, but two people were cleaning out his house. I asked for the man's whereabouts and they informed me that he had died. I inquired about other members of the family, and one of them said that the old man had a son who lived overseas somewhere, but that he hadn't been back to the states for years.

Frustrated, I asked if they knew what bank the old man used. The spokesman thought it was a certain Mellon branch but, when I went there, the manager told me that the key came from a different branch. I found it, signed the signature card, showed my ID, explained the problem, and waited while the service rep made a phone call. At last I was allowed into the vault; I found box 4037, opened it, and removed a single envelope. Deciding to extend the suspense a bit longer, I drove home with it so that I could open the envelope in front of the whole family.

I laid it on the table during dinner, causing no end of speculation. We hurried through the meal because the suspense was killing all of us. After one of Audrey's apple pies had been consumed, it was finally time. Slitting the envelope with my pie-smeared dinner knife, I pulled out a single sheet of paper. I held it up for all to see, showing them that there was another safety deposit key taped to the bottom. This one was stamped with the number 2434. The letter was addressed to "Herbert." It read:

Dear Herbert,

As promised, the key we have often spoken of is now in your possession since you have reached your 25th birthday. I hope by now you have forsworn your foolish ways and have decided to act like the mature man I have always hoped you would one day become.

This key is symbolic – it is the key to your future and it will unlock your true character. It will open to you a choice between short-term greed and life-long treasure.

You have always resented my wealth, at the same time hoping that it would one day become yours. But wealth without discipline is both meaningless and destructive. This key will give you the opportunity to demonstrate whether you have the personal discipline to manage part of my estate.

Follow my instructions, rein in your impatience, and you will be satisfied with the result. Ignore what I now tell you, grab what you can in your usual greedy frenzy, and you will be sadly disappointed.

I am dealing with this matter in this way because I will not be here by the time you turn 25. I trust that my faith in your ability to change will be justified. I wish you a fruitful and constructive life and I remain, your loving aunt,
Harriette M. McC.

I looked at the family and they looked at me. Jessica asked, "Can I see it?" I handed it to her and she examined it, commenting on the pretty handwriting. We discussed the next step for several days before I phoned the Post-Gazette and asked for the obituary desk. I got the name of the funeral home which had handled Mr. Marchand's arrangements and called them. The funeral director informed me that Mr. Herbert Marchand had only one relative, a son also named Herbert who had worked in the oil fields in Saudi Arabia. Their information indicated that he had been killed in an industrial accident a month earlier. The director suspected that the loss of his son had contributed to Mr. Marchand's death. I asked about Harriette M. McC. He said, "Yes, we list the deceased's sister as Harriette Marchand McCartney. She died in 1974." When I double checked, he assured me that Mr. Marchand had had no living relatives.

"Well," I said to anyone who was listening, "I guess that means the key belongs to us. Let's go see what this one produces."

I had to go to several branches before I found a manager

who recognized the key as belonging to his bank. Annabelle was with me this time. I fit the key into the safety deposit lock, removed the tray, which was quite heavy, and laid it on the pullout shelf. When I opened the top, we saw several kraft envelopes with button-and-string ties. There was a name neatly printed on the front of each envelope. Anna's eyes danced as she pulled one of them out of the tray.

"Can I open it?" she begged. "Please! I can't wait." I nodded. She undid the tie, carefully peered inside, then looked at me, her eyes wide. "It's money!" She reached in and discovered a stack of hundred dollar bills about a quarter of an inch thick. She counted them carefully, brand new stiff bills that were hard to separate, then handed them to me and said, "Fifty of them. $5,000! Holy cow. We're rich!"

Grabbing another envelope from the tray, she opened it and found the same thing, $5,000 in hundred dollar bills. She let out a little high-pitched girlish squeal and asked, "What are we going to get with all this money?"

I reminded her that there were names on all the envelopes, and we had to find out what that meant. When I lifted the rest of the envelopes out of the tray, I found underneath them a white envelope on which was written the name "Herbert." I told Annabelle, "This probably contains the instructions she mentioned in the other letter. We'll have to wait 'til we get home and decide what we're supposed to do with all this...stuff." Anna squealed again, danced a little jig, and gave me a powerful hug. I had to admit, it was pretty exciting.

The family gathered around the dining room table when we got home, and each one of them took one of the envelopes and opened it. I was amused to see everyone busily counting hundred dollar bills. We looked like a scene from one of those gangster films where the robbers are greedily counting their loot after a bank job.

I said in a loud gangster voice, "Nobody leaves da room widdout bein' frisked!" Then I added, "This is not our money...yet. Remember that. We have to read the instructions." I opened the white envelope and read the letter to them.

Dear Herbert,

You are now in possession of $35,000, more money than you have ever seen at one time. I am entrusting it to you with the stipulation that you follow my instructions exactly. As I said in my previous letter, if you give in to greed and fail to do as I say, you will be sadly disappointed.

The names on the envelopes are those of people with whom I worked in France during the late war. They are in need of help. You are now in a position to help them. I want you to deliver the seven envelopes to the people noted on each one, whose addresses are printed below. When you speak to each one, you will ask this question: 'What is your number?' Each one will give you a single digit. The envelopes are marked in order from #1 through #7. It is essential that you visit these people in that order. *If you do not, my plan will not work. When you have delivered all seven envelopes and collected all seven numbers, you will put the numbers in the sequence* in which you obtained them, *and then decide what your next move should be.*

Again, I trust you to behave like a mature adult in this enterprise. If you do, you will be satisfied with the results. If you do not, you will be sadly disappointed.

Your loving aunt,
Harriette M. McC.

Joey laughed. "Wow! We have a real whodunit here! Cloak and dagger stuff."

"I feel bad for Herbert," Audrey said. "It doesn't sound like old Aunt Harriette had a very high opinion of him. I wonder what he did to get on her bad side. And how did she make all her money?"

"Probably inherited it," chimed in Jessica.

I said, "Suppose each one of you writes down the address on your envelope. Who has #1?"

"I do," said Raymond.

"OK, what's the name?"

"Lucy Allard."

"Here's the address for #1," I said. "It's on Ayrshire Road in Monroeville."

Ray carefully wrote it down on the envelope. "But," he protested, "are we just going to give all this money away? To people we don't even know?"

The expressions on the faces of the rest of them were asking the same question. "This is our money," Anna added. "We have it in our hands right here. It would really help with my college fund. We could do all sorts of things with it."

"When's the last time you had $35,000 all at one time?" Jess asked, giving me an intense look.

I nodded. "I know, it feels like it's ours. But you have to remember some things. I was ready to hand the key back to the old guy who sold us the car. There was a question about whether it was really ours. And the letter from Aunt Harriette makes it clear we have a choice between a little profit now and something even better later on."

"But how do we know that's true?" asked Ray. "She could be lying to us, trying to trick us."

I reminded them, "These seven people are in need. We can help them...if we do the right thing."

Joey grunted. "If they're in such need, how come she didn't give them the money directly instead of playing this kind of mind game with us?"

"Good question," I admitted. "I think it's some kind of a test. I want to see where it leads us. She's warned us twice now about being greedy. By grabbing this money, we could be missing out on something even better."

They all sat playing with the wads of cash in their hands, and then, one by one, stuffed the bills back into the little brown envelopes.

Audrey and I drove to the house in Monroeville the next Saturday. Lucy Allard was a short woman about sixty years of age. She had brightly colored orange/blond hair and bright intelligent eyes to match. She smiled at us through the glass of her storm door.

"Can I help you?" She had a French accent, just like old Herbert.

"We are friends of Harriette Marchand McCartney, and we have a gift for you."

She eyed us suspiciously for a while, then said, "Harriette is dead. Is this some sort of trick?"

"No, no, I assure you," I said hastily, "we're not trying to trick you. She left some money for you before she died and asked us to deliver it. And also I need to ask, 'What is your number?'"

At that she reacted oddly, jumping backward and reflexively covering her hands. She started to close the front door, but I pulled out the letter and held it up to the storm door window. "Is this Harriette's signature and handwriting?" I asked.

She examined it for a moment, and then called something back into the house. She was soon joined by a large, rather fearsome looking man. We just stared at each other for a moment, and then she opened the door. Once inside, I tried to explain the strange events of the past weeks. Lucy told us that she and Harriette had known each other in Paris during the war, but wouldn't say what kind of activity they were involved in. I guessed that they were part of the Resistance, but nothing was mentioned about that.

I held out the kraft envelope, which she opened. When she pulled out the stack of bills, her husband gasped. "What is this?" she asked in confusion.

"Something Harriette wanted you to have."

She looked at the money and then at us. "And why are you doing this? What do you stand to gain?"

"Nothing," I told her. "Nothing, except we are supposed to ask, 'What is your number?'" She had the same odd reflexive reaction, hiding her hands in her lap.

After a moment she relaxed slightly. "I'm sorry," she said. "It's a habit from many years. Why do you want my number?"

"I don't know," I confessed with a shrug. "It's what Harriette told us to do after we distribute all the envelopes."

She looked at us as though she still didn't trust us. "How many others are there?" I told her there were six. She nodded finally and said, "Ah, yes. She is paying her bills." She continued to nod as if she were conducting some kind of inner dialog.

"We should be going," I said. "All we need is the number."

Lucy stood and walked over to me. Holding out her left hand, she spread her thumb and first finger, revealing the web of skin between them. There, on the inside, was a tiny tattoo of the number seven.

On the way home, we realized how exhausting the visit had been – tense and suspicious. Very odd. We agreed that we wouldn't have made very good spies. As a result, we took our time making the other six calls. It was two months later that we visited the last person. His name was Jacques Charron and he lived in a rather run down section of Wilkinsburg. He was elderly but he greeted us warmly when we mentioned Harriette's name.

"How is my dear old friend?" he asked in the same subtle French accent as the rest of the seven.

He held the door open for us and, as we sat in his cramped living room, I asked, "Didn't you hear that she died several years ago?"

"Ah," he responded. "Poor soul. Perhaps I did hear. I don't remember things so good anymore."

We handed him the envelope with the usual explanation, and he peered inside without emotion. "Ah," he said, nodding, "she said she would. Good old friend."

"She asked us to ask you, 'What is your number?'" I said.

He didn't change his expression, but he made the same motion with his hands, as if covering them up. "What number would that be?" he asked warily.

I was accustomed to this response by now. "The one by your thumb on your left hand," I said.

"Ah, *that* one," he said quietly. "You know about that number."

"Yes," I told him. "We've talked to the other six people in your group and they all gave us their numbers."

He nodded. "Ah, yes, the six others. They are all well?"

"Yes," I assured him, "all quite well. You French folks live long and healthy lives."

He continued nodding, but added, "It was not always so."

As we started to leave, I asked if I could see his left hand. Inside the wedge of skin between thumb and forefinger was the tattoo, the number eight.

At home, we sat down in the evening with the whole family. "Well," I said, "we've distributed all the money and gotten all seven numbers. What do we do now?"

Annabelle piped up. "When we were in the bank, I said to

you we're rich. Now we're poor again. What was the point of all that?"

I ignored her and said, "Let's put the numbers together." I pulled out our notes and had everyone write them down in the proper order, as Harriette had instructed us, from the first to the seventh visit.

After we arranged them properly, I asked, "Now what are we supposed to do?"

Ray scribbled for a moment, then said, "They total 36. Maybe that means something."

"It means you can't add," said Joey, with a laugh. "They really add up to 39." Ray made a face and punched his brother on the arm.

"Maybe it's the combination of the lock on a safe or a locker somewhere," said Anna.

"But where?" everyone chimed in.

We thought for awhile. "Bank account number?" "Lottery ticket number!?" We were getting nowhere. We broke up and decided to talk more about it at dinner. At some point Joey, noticing that the first three numbers were 793, got out the phonebook, then hollered for me.

"Hey, Dad, there's a 793 phone exchange in Pittsburgh. Maybe it's a phone number."

"Good idea," I said, grabbing the phone. I dialed in the seven numbers after the area code, and waited almost breathlessly. It rang! Three rings, four rings, and then a man's voice almost shouted, "Hello?"

"Hello," I said. "Who's this?"

He didn't answer my question. "How did you get this number?" he asked urgently.

"Harriette Marchand McCartney gave it to me."

A long silence. Then he said with a chuckle, "I've been waiting two years for this phone to ring. I almost had a heart attack just now!" I had no idea what he was talking about, but he said, "I think you had better come see me. The sooner, the better."

He was a lawyer with an office in Cranberry Township, north of Pittsburgh. He gave me his address, and the next day Audrey and I sat down with him.

"How did you get involved in this whole business?" he asked. "You're not French, and you're not Herbert, Jr."

I explained, "I found the first key in the back of an old car I bought from the elder Herbert. I tried to find the owner of the key but everyone's dead. So I concluded it was ours. Am I right, or does it belong to Harriette's estate?"

"No, you're right. The estate goes to the person who presents me with the second key, providing that the terms of the agreement have been carried out. I presume you've distributed the seven envelopes or you wouldn't have found the phone number and been able to contact me."

"Right," I said. "We handed out the $35,000 just like Harriette instructed us to, although my kids thought I was insane to give it all away."

He chuckled. "You're far from insane. You *would* have been if you'd kept that money, because that would have been the end of it. She didn't intend for it to end this way, with someone other than her nephew being the beneficiary; the money was for him. He turned twenty-five two years ago, and I've been waiting for him to use that key ever since. But I have the discretion to disburse the funds, and since you've done what she asked you to do, I am considering you her honorary nephew. So…I have something for you." He handed me a sheet of paper covered with legalese. It made no sense except for a figure that was prominent in the middle, the number $560,000.

"What's this?" I asked.

"That, sir, is what that second key is worth. Do you have

the key?"

I fumbled for it and, for a moment, couldn't find it. I panicked, then felt it in my pocket. "I don't understand," I said. "Why all this money?"

"You, sir, are a very lucky man," he responded. "Harriette was very fond of Herbert, Jr. She had no children and he was her only nephew. She married a steel millionaire and was worth a lot of money, but she had no family to spend it on except her nephew. However, he was a total wastrel and she was disgusted with him. She never gave up on him, though, and thought that this might be a way to make him grow up. But they all died and you stumbled into a fortune."

"How do you suppose the key got in that old car, stuck under the floorboards?"

"Maybe Herbert, Sr. hid it there; he was holding it for his son's 25th birthday. Or maybe it just fell out of his pocket. Or maybe your guardian angel slipped it in when you weren't looking. I have no idea. And I wouldn't try too hard to find out. Just…take the money and run."

I couldn't contain my curiosity. "Why all this cloak and dagger stuff? Why didn't she just leave the money for him in the safety deposit box?"

He smiled at some private joke. "Well, let's just say that Harriette was a rather…unusual person. She had been involved in some sort of special activities during the war, and she was a very secretive and suspicious sort of personality. She was used to codes and mystery, and I guess she couldn't break the habit. And for her it was a kind of game, the sort of amusement that rich people can afford. Of course, she also wanted to make sure that the money didn't fall into the wrong hands."

"Well, it did, didn't it?"

He shook his head. "I don't think she would have been upset by your discovery. She would have admired your ability to crack the code, so to speak. Because," he added, "she thought that if Herbert, Jr. couldn't figure it out, he didn't deserve the money anyway."

"And all of the other people, how did they happen to be here, too?"

"She brought all of them over here ten years ago when she found out they were poor and alone, and she set them up with homes and employment. She felt responsible for them because of their work together during the war."

"What would have happened," I asked him, "if we had kept the $35,000 and not distributed it?"

"Well," he said, "you would have been a lot poorer than you are right now."

"I mean, what about the seven people who needed the money she specified for them? They wouldn't have gotten anything?"

"Oh, quite the contrary," he laughed. "They would have split the 560 grand. Since Herbert, Jr. is dead, I was waiting to distribute the money to them. But I had to wait until the way was clear to bring his body home for identification. Another week or so and the money would have been gone! So, good timing on your part!" Then he added with a laugh, "That's why your phone call was such a shock. It was a dedicated line for Herbert, Jr. I thought I was getting a call from a ghost!"

I laughed along with him, but something was bothering me. "So, we're denying them that money?"

"Oh, no," he said with a shake of his head. "She had a lot more money than you're getting. They'll be well taken care of."

"What was the story about the eight of them, anyway? Were they in the French Resistance together?"

"What resistance?" he asked innocently. "Which eight people are you referring to? I have no idea what you're talking about. We never had this conversation and you, sir, were never in this office. And now that the key has been returned to me, I can finally take this damned telephone off my desk. One call on it in the five years since her death, and it's cost a fortune in monthly fees. Now, let's do some paperwork."

At home that evening, I explained what was to become of our windfall. I planned to set up four accounts for the children with $100,000 in each one, available to them when they turned eighteen. As for the other $160,000, I was going to get us out of debt, give $25,000 to Habitat for Humanity, take Audrey on a second honeymoon, and bank the rest for our retirement.

And, oh yes, later on I took the 1942 Chevrolet Aerosedan to the best antique car restoration company I could find and spent $15,000 on a total rebuild, which helped me to win Best in Class at the 1983 car show in Hershey, PA. Today it's better than new and worth $25,000. It took a while, but that thirteen-year-old boy's automotive dream finally came true.

Ain't she purty?

IV

<u>Merlen</u>

It's 2008, I'm fifty-six years old, and I'm still in love with a girl I first saw when I was fourteen. There's no fool like an old fool.

My parents owned a rental cottage right on the beach in Cape May, New Jersey, and we spent a week there every August. We made that annual pilgrimage from the time I was born through my junior year in high school. My two older brothers were always willing to go, because they could spend the week together chasing chicks, while I was stuck with my parents. So, by the time I was fourteen, I hated the place. I begged them not to make me go. There was nothing to do but lie on the beach and get sunburned. I was too young to join my brothers in chasing girls but, in my case, that would have been a waste of time anyway.

To be honest, if you'd have looked up the word "geek" in the dictionary, my photo would have been alongside the definition. I was 6' tall and weighed 115 pounds. I had no chest and my upper arms were the size of chopsticks. I had tight curly hair that looked like a sponge sitting on top of my head, and I wore thick glasses that made me look cross-eyed. And I got good grades in school. That was the worst demerit. I was smart, but the guys in school didn't like smart. They liked macho and I didn't qualify. So I was on the outside of everything, including getting any kind of attention from the girls. They just looked at me and laughed.

Jenny and I dated, more out of desperation than any real affection. We were both at the bottom of our respective D-lists, so we were perfect for each other. She had pimples, a big nose, wore glasses, and was so shy she couldn't look you in the eye. Well, she could look *me* in the eye because we were used to each other. She lived around the corner from me and we had known each other since kindergarten. As we got older, we were sort of thrown together all the time because there *was* no one else, and because we were two souls sharing the same excruciating experience in school. We understood each other, we were familiar, comfortable, the kind of company that misery loves. Dating her proved to the rest of the world what a loser I was, but it worked both ways. She must have been humiliated that I was the only guy she could catch.

It was 1966. I had finished my freshman year in high school and was going to turn fifteen in a month. As my mother started the annual process of packing up the family for another week at the shore, I started my campaign to be released from this annual imprisonment. My brothers, both of whom were in college, were free to roam the beaches on their own, whereas I was still tied to my parents' coattails like some little kid. I was sick of doing jigsaw puzzles, playing cards and making the mandatory morning and afternoon visits to the ocean. My parents didn't swim, my brothers were nowhere to be seen, so I had no one to swim with and I was too old to build sandcastles. I begged for weeks to be allowed to stay home with my one guy friend and, amazingly, I finally extorted a promise from my mother. If *next* year I still didn't want to go, she would see what arrangements could be made. It wasn't much, but it was at least a ray of hope.

We arrived at our cottage late on a Saturday afternoon. I had been sandwiched between my brothers in the backseat of the car, enduring hours of kidding and having to listen to their delicious plans for the week, which I wouldn't be able to share. I was almost glad when we arrived so I could get away from them. I was assigned the top of one of the bunk beds while they took both bottoms. I didn't mind, because I practically had the room to myself since they were gone most of the time. We unloaded, ate, and went to the beach in the evening, setting up chairs in which to sit and look at the waves. I had seen the waves. Many times.

The next morning I tried a new tack. I asked my mother if I could go up the beach some little distance from where they always planted their chairs. When she said a reflexive no, I started my usual whining – my brothers were gone all day, I was almost fifteen, it was time to cut me a little slack, etc. She glanced at Father, looked at me thoughtfully and – miracle – said OK. "But I want you within sight!"

A baby step toward independence, toward making this week a little more tolerable. I was ecstatic. I grabbed my towel and trotted north on the packed sand, knowing exactly where I wanted to go. That stretch of the beach terminated in a little cove surrounded by an outcropping of rocks that ran down to join the remains of an old breakwater. The formation created a private little beach which was usually uninhabited. I would be visible from where my parents were sitting, but far enough away to feel some sense of independence.

Spreading my towel, I lay down with my feet toward the ocean. It was early enough in the morning that the sun hadn't yet heated the sand. The breakwater interrupted the surf so that all I could hear was the lapping of tiny waves against the old stone wall. The curve of the rock formation insulated me from the sound of the breakers, and in my cozy nook I began to doze off, dreaming about being grown, getting my driver's license, bulking up. And becoming irresistible to girls.

I was facing north so I wouldn't have to look in the direction of my mom and dad, but my left cheek started to get chilled from the damp sand. So I turned my head to the other side, toward where they were sitting a hundred yards down the beach. And got the shock of my life!

There was a girl sitting on a blanket not ten yards away, between me and my parents. I was paralyzed with surprise. I hadn't counted on anything like this. Where had she come from? I hadn't heard her approaching or getting settled. Here I was, all alone, with no idea of the proper protocol in a situation like this, and no one to clue me in.

Of course, I made believe I didn't see her at first. That way I couldn't be blamed for making a wrong move. I closed my eyes tightly so she might think I was just asleep. But then I began tiny experiments: how much could I see through the smallest possible opening of my eyelids? Maybe just one eye would be safer. The problem was that this made her appear to be at right angles to me, so I couldn't get a clear picture of what she looked like.

I did my best with what little I could see. She appeared to be a couple of years older than me. She had long dark hair, smooth and shiny, that hung down to the middle of her back. She was wearing a modest one-piece bathing suit, not a bikini like lots of the girls had started to wear. It was dark blue with various different colors running through it. The contrast made her skin look very white, even though she appeared to have a light suntan. She wasn't wearing sunglasses so I could see her profile quite clearly at that distance, and it was obvious that she was very pretty. In fact, beautiful.

She sat facing out to sea without moving, not acknowledging my presence. I was in a huge turmoil about how to deal with this state of things. She had certainly seen me when she decided to put her beach towel down in this spot. She was close enough to have established a connection with me, but far enough away so that she wasn't in my space. Did that invite an opening on my part, or signal that she wanted to be left alone? I couldn't decide.

I noticed that she didn't have any of the equipment that girls usually find necessary at the beach – radio, suntan lotion, purse, book, etc. Her large beach towel, which was decorated with different colored stripes that coordinated with her bathing suit, was empty. Except for her.

She leaned back with her arms behind her, her legs flat on the blanket, her toes tilted slightly forward. I could see she had a perfect figure, slim but not skinny. The way she was sitting, I could see the outline of her breasts perfectly. I was grateful for the distance between us, because I was sure she couldn't see me staring greedily at her. She was so beautiful. And I was going nuts trying to decide what to do.

I closed my eyes again because I was already burning up with fantasies about her. I peeked at her every once in a while to refresh my memory of the details that I liked the best, and then went back to my imaginary interactions with her. But the third or fourth time I cracked my eyelids to take another squint, she was gone!

I sat up with a jolt. I hadn't heard her leave just as I hadn't heard her arrive. What was going on here? Where could she disappear to so quickly? There didn't seem to be a natural exit over the rocks, and I would certainly be able to see her if she walked away in the direction from which I had come. She had been there only about fifteen minutes. Why such a short time?

That night in our room, I mentioned to the guys that I had seen a pretty girl on the beach that morning, that she had come down to sit close to me. But saying anything to them was a bad mistake. They laughed at the idea, asked if I had made a move on her, then told me they were going to come tomorrow and take turns ravishing her there in front of my eyes. It was obvious afterward that I could never mention her again.

I could hardly sleep that night for thinking about her. When I did sleep, dreams about her would wake me in a sweat. I practiced a dozen opening lines on her, but couldn't decide which one to use. Some advice from my brothers would have been helpful, but I didn't dare ask. So I was exhausted the next morning when I hurried back to my spot, hoping to see her again. This time I lay on my back to get a better view, but I was so tired I fell asleep.

I woke, having dreamt of her again, turned my head, and there she was. Same place, same towel, same absence of clutter around her. Same position, leaning back, looking out to sea. Same bathing suit, too. The only difference was her hair. Today it was pulled together in a long ponytail which hung slightly away from her body, just touching the towel.

I looked at her a little more openly this time hoping that, if she glanced my way, I might find the courage to say something. But she just stared into the distance as she had the previous day. That gave me the boldness to check her out a little more carefully. I guessed she might be seventeen or eighteen. She had a pretty profile, a pert, attractive little nose and a cute chin. I wondered what it would be like to trace that profile with my fingertip.

This time I was determined to stay awake so I could see where she disappeared to. But as I stared at her, trying to fill my brain with every detail, my vision seemed to freeze-frame, so that what I was seeing was not the present moment but the image already in my mind. As a result, when my senses finally cleared, she was gone again. That was twice I had lost her. I couldn't seem to force myself to stay awake.

I was afraid to mention her to anyone after the bad experience I had had with my brothers. But I did hazard a comment to my mother. "Did you see anyone else down in that cove where I was lying this morning?"

She thought for a moment, then said, "No, I really wasn't paying attention." I knew that wasn't true since she had been keeping a rather keen eye on me. But apparently she hadn't noticed my girl.

My life was consumed with wondering about her. I looked for her everywhere we went – bicycling on the boardwalk, at the zoo, Cold Spring Village or the lighthouse. I wondered what her name might be, where she lived, what grade she was in, why she only seemed to come to that one spot. My parents sensed my distraction, but wrote it off to my not wanting to be there. How wrong they were!

On the third morning, I went down to my spot by the breakwater again, determined this time to make some kind of bold move, even if it killed me. But I had begun to have funny thoughts about the whole business. I knew it wasn't a dream, but it was almost as though my fantasies had brought her to life, like she was some projection of my frustration with myself. It seemed that on that piece of beach, when I closed my eyes for a moment, I went into an altered state which made it possible for her to appear to me. So I decided I would give that theory a test.

I lay down on my stomach, turned to face her spot, closed my eyes and tried to meditate for a couple of minutes. I visualized her, saw every detail of her and her towel and bathing suit, even tried to see the wind blowing her hair. I got so caught up in the mental image that I suddenly realized I hadn't actually looked for her. So I opened my eyes. And there she was.

Now I was really confused. Was I dreaming this? Was she just a figment of my imagination? Was I somehow generating her out of thin air? Was I losing my mind? The perplexing thing about it was that she always looked the same – seemingly unaware of my presence, leaning back on her hands, looking toward the ocean, her legs flat on the blanket, never moving, identical to the day before. Except that her hair was different again. This time it was in one long braid which hung down behind her, its wispy tip just touching the towel. That difference gave me hope that I wasn't inventing this whole thing. I hadn't imagined her with different hairstyles every day.

Was this the time to make my move? I started to sit up a dozen times, but my muscles wouldn't work. So I tried to recall my clever pickup lines, but none of them would come to me. Then I got to thinking – after three days, it's a little late to start now. She'll wonder why I didn't say something the first day. She'll think I'm some klutzy loser who doesn't know how to act around girls. Why do I want to talk to her anyway? Am I going to ask her for a date? I almost laughed out loud when I thought about that. All I'm doing is asking for more rejection and humiliation. So I just went on lying there. Looking at her. And then...

She turned and looked at me.

Panic! My throat closed up and I couldn't breathe. I thought I was going to suffocate. I watched her gather herself, rise, pick up her towel and give it a little shake, then turn in my direction. From my angle on the ground, I could see her bare feet moving toward me, and for the first time I noticed her red toenail polish. When she stopped ten feet away, I finally found the strength to push myself up and look at her.

She was so much prettier, standing there facing me. I wanted to get up, because I felt like a fool lying there in a kind of collapsed push-up position. But I didn't have the strength. She looked down at me without any expression and, in a soft voice, said, "I was waiting for you to say hello." She held my eyes with hers for a brief moment longer, then turned and walked away. Although I wanted to watch her go, I couldn't bear to do it.

I was staggered, frozen in place, completely unable to think or move, my senses totally maxed out. I knew I had looked and acted like a damned fool, that I had just blown the best opportunity of my whole life. I collapsed on the towel, more upset with myself than I had ever been. I walked slowly back to the cottage, kicking myself every step of the way. I would never see her again, this beautiful creature who had been waiting all week for me to talk to her.

I wasn't surprised when she didn't appear the next morning. She had given me a chance and I had blown it big time. I didn't go back the remaining mornings because it was just too painful to think about. And then the week ended.

Back home, I started a private journal specifically about Her. I had decided that any name I might give her would not do justice to the vision I had seen, so I decided to just call her "Her." I wrote down a comprehensive description of her, with the most minute details I could come up with, as well as others I could only imagine in my teenage fantasies. I started to invent a history for her, complete with family relationships, hobbies, favorite things and school activities. Then abruptly I tore those pages out, realizing that my imagination could only diminish her, since nothing I might think of could possibly equal the truth.

Over the following year, I wrote her many letters, trying to offset the stupid behavior I had exhibited when she spoke to me. I also wrote a kind of wordplay, complete with dialog from imagined conversations with her, practicing for the next time I saw her. If I ever did. And when I dated Jenny, I tried to imagine that Her was at my side in the movies. It was an illusion which I could maintain only if I never looked at Jenny, which didn't do much for the quality of our date. But that fantasy never worked anyway, because Her was shapely and tall while Jenny was short and sort of chubby.

When our sophomore year English teacher assigned us to write a character description of a person living, dead or imaginary, I went at it with such a passion that I got an A+. But I had screwed myself, because the teacher thought it was so good that she demanded that I read it to the class. It was humiliating in the extreme, an invasion of my privacy. The boys made endless fun of me, assuming that she was someone I had done "it" with last summer, and turning my story into something nasty. The girls, on the other hand, came up to me babbling about how they wished someone would write things like that about them. But that's as far as it went. I felt like Cyrano, writing things that turned women on to other men.

The year dragged because, for once, I wanted to go back to Cape May. When the time approached, my mother, true to her promise, asked if I wanted to be excused. I tried to restrain myself so she wouldn't catch on to my ulterior motive. She actually tried to talk me out of going, and I had a sudden panic attack that I would be left behind.

But we ended up there again on a Saturday afternoon in August, just the three of us, since the boys both had jobs which required them. Mother urged me to stay near the cottage, but I managed to get away and hurried to visit the cove. I looked for footprints, impressions of a towel in the sand, even sniffed the air trying to catch the scent of her. But there was nothing.

The next morning, my parents went to visit an old friend in Wildwood, just up the coast from Cape May. They demanded that I go along, of course, and we had a huge fight about it. But they absolutely forbade me from staying there alone, saying that Mrs. Whatserface would be hurt if I didn't come. I had no choice. The morning was torture and we didn't get back til 3:00. By then, everything was wrong and I knew she wouldn't appear. I waited by our spot til supper with growing despondency.

Monday morning, I carried my camera down to the cove determined to capture my prey one way or another. I lay down on the sand, meditated – prayed, really – and waited to see whether it would happen again, whether perhaps I could make her appear by the sheer force of my desperation to see her. When I figured I was in the proper state of being, I peeked off to the side.

She was there!

I sat up instantly and faced her. She was sitting on the same towel, wearing the same bathing suit, holding the same pose. But her hair was loose again, hanging down her back, lovely, long, shiny and dark. She hadn't changed a bit and, if I blinked, I could swear it was still last year. But I didn't dare blink because I was sure I would jinx the moment and she would vanish before my eyes.

I called, "Hi," which was the best I could do for an opening gambit.

She turned and looked at me, but said nothing. In another moment, she was back looking out to sea. I got up and walked over to her. "I was hoping to see you again this year," I said tentatively. "I didn't know if you'd be here again or not."

"I'm always here." She glanced up at me with no particular expression.

"Where do you live?" I asked.

She slowly turned her gaze back to the horizon. "Here," was all she said.

I started several sentences, but got tongue-tied and stopped. Being this close to her was far too stimulating. I was desperate to look at her close up, and she didn't appear to mind since she never took her eyes off the water. She was very pretty, with dark brown eyes, fine eyebrows, a delicate, very feminine nose, and exquisite skin. I felt like a troll standing in the presence of a princess. Since I knew there was no real future for me here, I decided I had better get what I had come for and get out.

"Can I take your picture?" I asked, with an awkward hint of pleading in my voice.

She didn't say no. What she did say was, "You won't capture the real me."

I didn't know what she was talking about, and I didn't care. I took one picture of her looking east, and then asked her to look at me. She slowly turned her face toward me. "Smile!" I said. But she didn't. I waited, then figured I had better shoot her before she turned away again.

"Are you going to be here tomorrow?" I asked.

"I'll be here." She said it very softly.

I was a nervous wreck and was running out of things to say, but the awkwardness of the situation didn't seem to touch her at all. "Can I ask your name?" I said.

She didn't answer for a moment, then looked up at me again. "Merlen."

"Like the wizard," said I, brilliant conversationalist that I was.

"No," she said after a bit. "M-e-r-l-*E*-n."

"Oh," I said, as another wave of stupid washed over me. "Well, goodbye. Thanks for the photo." She didn't respond. I went back to my place in the sand, but by then the gongs and fireworks were going off so loudly in my head that I couldn't see or hear a thing.

I thought a dip might clear my mind, and might also impress her with my macho-ness. So I ran into the water and dove into the first wave I could find, head first. *God!* It was like ice. I thought I was going to die! But I had to tough it out for the benefit of my audience. Trying not to let her see the agony on my face, I kept my back to her while I rubbed my arms to keep them from falling off. Assuming a pained smile, I turned in her direction. But, of course, she had disappeared.

On Monday afternoon, I took my pictures in to a FastFilm store to be developed. But when I went to get them the next morning, I was terribly disappointed. Though the other photos had come out clearly, the two pictures of her were foggy, as though my passion had steamed up the camera lens. Tuesday and Wednesday mornings found me flat on the sand again, meditating my brains out, but no Merlen. I prowled the boardwalk for miles, but never did see her. Then, on Thursday, I was walking by the community affairs office on the boardwalk, and stopped to glance at the things on the bulletin board out front. What I saw made my heart stop.

Pinned among the notices advertising all the current 1967 community events was a piece of red poster board on which someone had hand lettered the warning: *Don't Let This Happen To YOU!* Alongside the warning was a newspaper clipping with a headline that read, *Local Teen Caught in Riptide, Drowns.* And below the headline was her photo over the caption, *Merlen Robertson.* The shockwave that blasted through me left me so weak that I had to sit down. I made it back to the cottage, but by the time I got there I couldn't keep from crying. I explained the whole thing to my mother, who was properly sympathetic, and spent the rest of the day in bed.

On Friday morning, I went back to our spot, looking desperately for any sign of her final visit. But there was nothing. I sat there for a long time trying to decide how to say goodbye to her. Then it occurred to me – I would get a copy of the newspaper article. That would give me some information about her life and background, and also get me a photo of her since my own hadn't come out.

I went back to the community office and made my request. The woman behind the counter was very accommodating. She asked, "Did you know her?"

"A little," I said.

"It was so sad," she said, shaking her head. "She was such a beautiful girl." She brought out a huge scrapbook, went through the pages and found what she was looking for. She slid the article out of a sheet protector and put it in the copy machine. Then she carefully folded the copy, slipped it into an envelope, and handed it to me. "No charge," she said brightly.

I thanked her and walked back to the cottage rapidly. When I got there, I sat down on one of the bottom bunks, took out the article and read it carefully. It wasn't until I had gone through it a second time that I glanced at the dateline. The paper containing the article had been published on August 16, 1961.

V

Charlie

"Darkie kids are not proper playmates for you."
My father's comment was directed at me. He was holding
forth at the dinner table again. He often grilled us on our day's
activities, and then gave his considered opinion about every
aspect of our life – friends, activities, grades, you name it.

Dinner was a highly regimented affair. Dad had been a
colonel in the Marine Corps during World War II, and had been
awarded a bronze star for heroism in action on Iwo Jima. The
story was well known in our town and now, three years after
the war, people were still calling him "Colonel Shepardson."
He had become wealthy as president of his own construction
company in the Elizabeth area of New Jersey, and his
involvement in politics had made him a force in the
community. He was used to giving orders, and he was used to
being obeyed. And he expected his four boys to behave like
well-disciplined subordinates.

I was the second born and had been named Mark. My
parents were leaders in the Dutch Reformed Church, and it was
natural for them to give us Biblical names. Dad had been
determined to have four sons, although how he arranged it is a
mystery. I suppose he had simply confronted the good Lord
and given Him an order. He certainly had made it clear to my
mother that there were to be no girls in this family. In any
event, God had acquiesced and given them four sons. Matthew

(we didn't dare call him Matt) was thirteen and in eighth grade; I was eleven and in sixth. But Luke, who was eight, went to a special class for slow learners. My father always held it against God that He had given him a child with learning disabilities. To compensate, he was even harder on the rest of us when it came to our schoolwork. And, finally, his youngest son, John, was five and in kindergarten.

"My father used to call them pickaninnies, but I'm told that they don't like to be called that, just like they don't want you to call them 'n-----s'."

Looking back on it, I suppose that Dad considered himself open-minded and sensitive, since he was aware that certain ways of referring to "them" were offensive. It was 1948 and President Truman had just opened the way for the desegregation of the armed forces. My father was still dealing with the shock of that radical change in the traditions of the Corps, and was certain that his beloved Marines would go to hell in a hurry if "they" were allowed to don the uniform.

"They're different than we are," he was saying. "I saw them when I was aboard ship. They can handle menial work fine if you supervise them properly, but they haven't got the mental capacity to be officers, or even non-coms."

Dad sat with his back to the library shelves that filled one whole end of the dining room. Mommy sat at the opposite end, next to the kitchen door. Matthew and John sat on one side of the table, the baby next to Mommy, and Luke and I were on the other, with me closest to Dad. So, while he was directing his lecture to the family as a whole, my proximity to him allowed him to lean toward me in a conspiratorial attitude, with a tiny nod and a wink, as though to assure himself that I was getting the point.

"So," he went on, "it's really not appropriate to get too friendly with them since it's almost like they're from a different country, like we don't understand their language or their customs. They can't be part of our clubs or our churches, so it's not fair to give them false hopes that they can be like us. There's a reason why they live together on the south side. It's just better if we keep our distance. It makes everyone more comfortable."

Dad drew each one of us into the conversation, but we only spoke at the table when it was our turn. Since it was my report that had triggered this lecture, I had the privilege of following up on his comments.

"But we go to school with them," I ventured.

Dad nodded. "Yes, and that's because the law up here in the north requires that they go to school with our children. But the law doesn't say that we have to mix with them socially. They have their place and we have ours."

But I needed to point out something else. "Charlie lives right across the street from the school," I told him. "And there are white people's houses right down the road. He doesn't live where all the rest of the colored people do."

Dad gave a little frown. "I know," he said, "that's because his family was there long before the school was built. Those other houses just grew out toward where he lives and no one wanted to force them to move. But you've seen what that house looks like, haven't you?" I nodded. "Well, that shows you that they're different from us. You wouldn't want to live in a house in that condition, would you?" I shook my head slowly.

"Well," he said, taking a deep breath, "let's leave it that way. We'll stay in our place and let them stay in theirs."

My father had been inspired to share these comments with us by something I had said a few minutes earlier. When he asked me to report on what had happened at school, I was pleased to tell him about the highlight of my day, an important mission on which my teacher, Miss McKee, had sent me. I was thrilled that she had singled me out from the whole class and entrusted me with an errand which actually required me to leave the school building.

I was one of two boys in the sixth grade who had been chosen to be members of the student patrol. That meant that we arrived at school before the rest of the students were allowed in the building, that we went up to the third floor to put on our "uniform," which consisted of a metal medallion which we wore strapped to our right arm, and a white Sam Brown belt. Then the two of us were to station ourselves at either end of the building, open the doors when the bell rang, and keep order among the rush of kids filing into school. I had been assigned to supervise the girls' entrance, and I enjoyed being the only boy among all those little females. I was tall for my age and a member of the oldest class in the building, so I fancied that they all saw me as an older man with a lot of authority over them.

Since we were seated in alphabetical order and my name was Shepardson, I had to sit in the back row in the next to last seat in class. The only seat after mine, the one in the right rear corner of the room, was occupied by Charlie Vander.

Charlie was the only Negro boy in the school.

On this morning, Miss McKee was taking the roll; when she called my name, I answered "Here."

"Charlie." Silence. His seat was empty.

Miss McKee mumbled to herself, "Late again." Then to no one in particular, "Did anyone see Charlie this morning?" A general shaking of heads.

She went behind her desk and sat, pulling out a pad of paper and writing something. Then, without looking up, she said, "Mark!"

"Yes, ma'am."

"Come up here, please."

All heads turned in my direction. They knew I wasn't in trouble because I was the golden boy of the class. But they were curious. So was I.

Handing me the note, Miss McKee said, "Go across the street and see why Charlie isn't here. And show this note to the hall monitors." I started to leave, but she added, "Go in the cloak room and put on your patrol equipment."

So it was that I was liberated from Roosevelt School first thing in the morning; I was holding a pass which trumped the authority of the hall monitors, and was off to search for a fellow-student who had gone truant. Looking both ways, I crossed Springfield Avenue, dodging the traffic, and walked the two hundred yards to the Vander home.

Charlie lived in a house which had been built a very long time ago. I had walked by it many times, but always on the other side of the street. This was the first time I had been up close to it, and I noticed details I had never seen before. The place was badly in need of paint, and some of the siding was hanging at odd angles. A broken green rocking chair sat in the middle of the wide front porch, and the three dogs sprawled around it looked up at me with mild curiosity. There was no grass alongside a front walk which consisted of delaminated plywood sheets laid end to end. Mud was everywhere, and on its side by the porch steps lay the remains of an old tricycle. In a pile at one end of the porch, I noticed a dozen or more bags of what must have been garbage, judging from the squadrons of flies in formation around them. And at the front door lay an ancient mat, the encrusted mud all but obscuring its greeting: "Welcome."

I had the definite feeling of being in alien territory, about to enter a world so different from my own that I couldn't even imagine it. I realized that nothing in my past had even vaguely prepared me for this encounter. I rarely spoke to Charlie – no one did – and he spent his days sitting in his seat sort of huddled inside of himself. He almost never spoke in class, and yet he got almost all A's on his report card. This, to me, was an extraordinary phenomenon, and I realized that I was probably the only kid in class who knew about it.

I would share the occasional comment or joke with him, but for the most part he was totally cut off from the class, stuck in the corner farthest from the teacher's desk. Yet, on one or two occasions, he had flashed his report card at me after Miss McKee walked by passing them out. He knew that I was the smartest boy in the class, and I guess he felt that I would be the one person who could appreciate his accomplishment.

After the first grading period, he folded his card inside out so the grades were on the outside, then turned sideways in his seat and laid the card in his lap so it was shielded from everyone but me. He didn't say anything, merely waited until I glanced at him, then flicked his eyes downward to call my attention to his card. I studied it for a moment, then looked at him in wide-eyed astonishment. He smiled, refolded his card, slid it into its envelope, and put it away. I'm sure he figured I wouldn't tell anyone else, because they wouldn't want to believe he could do so well. And so it remained our secret. And Miss McKee's, because she never let on to the class that he was a good student. His perpetual silence misled everyone.

I raised my hand to knock on the door, but Charlie opened it. "I saw you coming," he said.

"Miss McKee sent me over to see why you're not in school."

A voice from inside called, "Who is it?"

Charlie turned and said, "Someone from school."

"Well, don't keep him standing there," the voice said. "Ask him to come in."

Charlie turned back and looked at me, letting the invitation hang in the air. When I backed away shaking my head, he asked in an amused tone, "You afraid?"

The challenge was like a punch in the face. I had never in the world figured on going into the house of black people. I had expected that I would merely stand at the door for a second, ask the question, and return to class. It suddenly occurred to me that I didn't know how long I had; when would Miss McKee be expecting me back? I didn't want to get into trouble by being gone too long.

But there was something else, something deeper. I had sat alongside Charlie all through sixth grade, and there was something of a silent companionship that had built up. I knew that he respected me, maybe even trusted me. But that classroom was *my* world. His shrunken, invisible presence in it testified to that. There was no doubt as to who was, and who was not, at home there.

Standing on his doorstep in this moment, however, made me realize with shock that I had left that world. I was suddenly in Charlie's world, a place as alien to me as that room full of white students must have been to him. I had no idea how to act or what to say. In a shattering moment of insight, I suddenly understood Charlie's silence.

"Well, are you?" He repeated the question.

I scrambled around in my brain for a response. "Uh, I think Miss McKee will be expecting me back." Charlie nodded, his mouth tightening slightly. "Are you sick?" I asked. "I have to tell her why you're not in school."

He paused. Drawing a breath, he said, "Somebody stole my shoes. I don't have no shoes."

I scowled in disbelief. "Who would do that?" He shrugged, showing no emotion except for a twitch at the corner of his mouth. "Don't you have other shoes?" I asked, giving him what seemed like the obvious solution.

His eyes fixed on mine. There was a long pause as though he was trying to figure out what I was thinking. At length he said, "I ain't got but the one pair." My eyebrows must have shot up in surprise because he went on: "I know you got a lot of shoes, but I ain't got but the one pair. And they're gone."

I didn't know what to say. I stared at him for a long moment, then asked the only thing I could think of: "Can't you come over in your bare feet?"

For the first time, I saw a flash of emotion in his face. "Yeah! And look like some kind of dumb n----r?"

I was so confused that all I could think of was escape. I mumbled a goodbye and stumbled off the porch in my hurry to flee the awkward situation. I ran across Springfield Avenue, flustered, my mind churning with conflicted feelings. I knew I had upset him, although that certainly hadn't been my intention. And I was angry with myself for the truth which he had revealed – I *had* been afraid to go into his house. And I was appalled at the idea that he thought he couldn't come to school because his only pair of shoes was missing.

I couldn't sleep that night. I rolled about trying to escape the troubling images and ideas that were the residue from my day. My father said Charlie and I should not be friends, and yet there was a unique bond between us – our shared secrets in the back of the room, our grades which put us both at the top of the class academically, although only the teacher and I were aware of that fact. And now I was the only person in the class who had set foot on his property and sensed that cultural divide first hand. What if I *had* gone through that door? What would I have seen?

Around midnight it all came together. The regret about showing my cowardice – what was there really to be afraid of? – the guilt about hurting Charlie's feelings in ways I didn't fully understand, and a growing curiosity about where he lived and what his world looked like beyond Room 36 in Roosevelt School. And then it hit me. He had said, with a kind of sad knowing that, although he had only one pair of shoes, I had many. That was it! Giving him a pair of my shoes would answer all of these regrets, and it would be a positive indication of friendship to a person who had few if any friends.

Now I was awake, pre-living the moment when I presented him with the gift – I saw him at the door, accepted his invitation to enter, offered him the paper bag enclosing the symbols of his freedom to return to class, watched the smile cross his face, and bowed my head humbly as his family approached and blessed me for my generosity. It was such an exciting scenario that I replayed it a dozen times, anxious for the morning to arrive. Eventually, it morphed into dream form and entertained me until the sun rose.

I need to confess here a life-long fear of authority stemming from the ways in which my father constantly intimidated us. He never truly left the Marine Corps, at least emotionally. It represented the highest achievements of his life, and had brought him the greatest recognition. He lived his life as if he had the starring role in a play called "The Colonel." He knew that it was discipline which had brought him safely back from the Pacific, and he figured that discipline would allow him to run his family in the most efficient way. No emotion, no softness, just duty, obedience and success. I hated him but I respected him. I felt safe around him…except when he thought I was in the wrong!

I never did anything without his permission. So, in my mind, giving those shoes away would impress him with my imagination and Christian generosity. But more than that, I felt that I could show my courage by bucking his authority; he respected courage. It was a very unusual thing for me to dream up and carry out a plan that he hadn't approved first. But my fear of his authority had run head-on into my conviction that, for the first time, he was wrong! He told me I couldn't be friends with Charlie. I knew that that attitude revealed his prejudice, and prejudice was wrong! I guess I wanted to prove something to him.

As soon as I was dressed the next morning, I rummaged through my closet looking for the perfect pair of shoes. I had six pairs – new sneakers, old sneakers, sponge-soled ties, black dress shoes, brown school shoes and beat-up old school shoes. My father made sure I kept the dress shoes polished. Sometimes I wore the brown shoes to school and sometimes I wore the sponge-soled ones, because the old school shoes, which were the most comfortable, were in such bad shape. But I hated the black dress shoes because they were new and stiff and hurt my feet. And I wore them only when I had to dress up, which I also hated. That was the pair my searching finger paused over.

I ran downstairs, took an empty grocery bag from Mommy's pile in the pantry, and put the shoes in it along with my school books. Mommy didn't seem to notice anything unusual, and I tried my best not to let her sense that something was up. I was so full of anticipation that I didn't want anything to interrupt my plan, realizing that parents can sometimes be funny about these things. So I managed to get out the house, hugging my package, and made it to school without having to share my plan with anyone, not even my friends. Because it occurred to me that some of them might think it was odd that I was planning to do something like this for...someone like Charlie.

As soon as I got to school, I ran into the classroom to get my patrol equipment. This gave me the chance to talk to Miss McKee. I explained my plan and she thought about it for a moment, then smiled and told me it was a very generous thing to do. She gave me permission to go to his house as soon as the students had entered the building and my patrol duties were completed.

I approached Charlie's house full of excitement but, as I got closer, the same sort of subtle anxiety crept in. What was I getting into? What would I say?

There was no one to greet me this time, and I had to knock on the door. Instead of Charlie, it was an old man with curly white hair who greeted me. He stared at me for a moment, then in a quiet voice said, "Yes?"

"Is Charlie here?" I asked him, my heart pounding so hard that it startled me. The old man turned and called something unintelligible back into the house.

Turning to me while we waited, he said, "You have to be good to your Mam and do what she tell you." I blinked in surprise, not certain I had heard him correctly. We stared at each other for a moment, and then Charlie appeared.

"You're here again" he observed. I nodded. Another awkward moment.

Finally I explained, "I have to check if you're coming back today."

He looked at me, an odd expression on his face, then said, "I still have the same problem as yesterday."

I blurted out, "That's why I came. I have something for you." He didn't know what to say – he was waiting for me to offer the gift, and I was waiting for him to invite me in. I was determined to go into his house this time, and I thought my gift gave me the perfect excuse to do so. Finally, I asked, "Can I come in? For a minute?"

He scowled ever so slightly, then said, "Yeah, sure." He stepped back and I edged my way around the old man who was still standing in the door. The main room had a wooden floor and wallpaper from which large sections were missing. The area was circled by what I gathered were old sofas, one on each wall, covered with blankets. Off to the left rear was the kitchen, and I could see a woman standing at a counter there, eyeing me curiously. Charlie led me into a room in the left front of the house, obviously a bedroom for more than one person. It had several beds in it and a mattress on the floor in one corner. He pointed to the mattress and said, "This is where I sleep. My sisters and my Mam and Poppa sleep there," indicating the beds.

I looked at his floor level sleeping area, and noticed behind his mattress a shelf filled with books. "Are those all yours?" I asked.

He nodded. "I read a lot when I'm not working. I get them from the library." Then, turning to me, he asked, "What do you have for me?" I held out the bag and he took it without looking at me. Opening it to peer in, he scowled again, then asked, still without looking at me, "What are these?"

Trying to minimize the gift, I said, "They're my old shoes." Immediately, I regretted the statement. First, they weren't old and, second, it sounded as though I was giving him junk. I hurriedly tried to cover my *faux pas* by saying, "Well, they're not really old," but he interrupted me.

"Why are you doing this?"

"So you can come back to school."

He looked me in the eye and said, in an ironic tone, "Thanks." At this moment, the old man, whom he called Poppa and who I judged to be Charlie's grandfather, wandered into the room. He looked at me with a curious smile and asked, "Are you one of the good boys?"

Again, startled, I wasn't sure how to react. "I hope so," I mumbled. Then turning to Charlie, I said, "I'd better get back to class." He saw me to the door and, as I left, I asked him, "Are you coming?"

He started back into the house and I heard him say, "Maybe later."

When I got home, I was anxious to tell my mother what I had done. But I was not prepared for her reaction. "You did *what*? You gave away your good new shoes without asking us? Your father is going to be very upset."

Suddenly, what I had done came crashing in on me. I had expected at least a little praise from my mother, thinking that she might temper my father's reaction. But it seemed that both of them were going to be angry with me. Still, I thought I had a reasonable defense in terms of helping a friend in need.

My father said nothing during dinner, but called me into his study as soon as the meal was over. Being called into the study was always an ominous thing, and I had not been able to eat much for worrying about it. He sat me down opposite his desk but pulled his chair around to face me.

"Now, tell me in your own words what you did today." His face was impassive, but I had seen that expression before.

"Charlie's a good student. He gets as good grades as I do. But he can't come to school because someone stole his shoes."

He waited, nodding. "Go on."

My heart was racing as I realized what I had to say next. I was desperate for him to understand my motivation. "He knew I had a bunch of shoes…and I found out he only had one pair."

"So he asked you for a pair of your shoes?" Dad's eyes drilled into me.

"No," I shouted. "I thought it was the Christian thing to do, to share with the poor. Isn't that what Jesus told us to do?"

With an icy quiet in his voice, he said, "It might have been what Jesus told us to do if you had given him your own shoes."

The statement was so unexpected and so confusing that I just looked at him with my mouth open. "But," I stammered, "I *did* give him my shoes."

Dad shook his head. "No," he said a little more sternly, "you gave him *my* shoes!"

I shook my head, completely puzzled. In almost a whisper, I said, "They weren't your shoes; they were my black dress ones."

He moved his chair a bit closer and leaned forward. "Did you buy those shoes?"

I scowled a bit. "No."

"No, because *I* bought those shoes. Did you ask me if you could give away those shoes that I bought for you?"

I suddenly saw where this was going. Deflated, I admitted that I hadn't asked for permission. I started to apologize but he cut me off. "So, what would you call this behavior of yours?" I didn't understand what he meant so I shook my head. "Well," he continued, "they were my shoes and you gave them away without my permission. What do you call that?"

"I don't know."

He moved even closer. "I call it theft!" he shouted.

I recoiled in shock. His words hurt worse than if he had slapped me in the face. I had wanted to do something nice, something in line with what I had been taught in Sunday School, but suddenly it had become a crime!

"And you gave them to a *black* boy!" he concluded, as if that were a crime even worse than theft. I started to cry. I couldn't help myself. "Tears won't get you out of this one, young man!" he said somewhat more quietly. Then after a moment he asked, "So, what shall we do about this?"

I couldn't think straight. I just shook my head and mumbled, "I don't know."

"Well, I'll tell you what *you're* going to do. You're going to talk to him tomorrow, and you're damned well going to tell him to give you back *my* shoes."

I looked at him in horror. "I can't do that!"

He flashed me a bitter smile and said, "Oh, yes you can. You are going to do just that."

I got no sleep that night. Between fits of crying and bouts of rage at my father, I tried to figure out what I could possibly say to Charlie tomorrow. I finally decided that the best solution was simply to run away somewhere. I never wanted to see my father again.

I walked into class the next morning, dreading what I would find. I peeked around the corner toward the rear of the room, and there sat Charlie at his desk next to mine. So, he had decided to use my gift and return to class. I walked to the back of the aisle and dropped into my seat. He didn't raise his eyes to meet mine. I glanced down to see my shoes, and sat up in shock! He was wearing a pair of very old, dirty brown shoes, obviously too large for him.

"Charlie," I called in a loud whisper. "Where did you get those shoes?"

"They're my Poppa's," he whispered.

"Where are the shoes I gave you?" He mumbled something and I had to ask him again.

He finally looked up and said, as if it made no difference at all to him, "My mother sold them."

I gasped for breath. That was the last thing in the world I expected to hear. "She *what*?" I said out loud. The whole class turned around to look at us. Charlie shriveled back inside himself and I turned around, too shocked to think straight. What was going to happen now? Did this get me off the hook? Would my father just forget about it now that the shoes were gone?

When school was over, I looked for Charlie but he was already gone. I thought about going over to see him but decided against it. I didn't know what to say to him. He obviously didn't think much of my gift to him.

I was called back into my father's study after supper. He resumed his place, his chair close in front of me, and leaned in as he asked, "Well, sir, let me hear what you did today to rectify this situation which you have created."

As I looked at him, I could feel the blood draining out of my face. "I couldn't get them back," I said in a tiny voice.

"You couldn't get them back," he repeated. "And just why was that?"

I took a deep breath. "His mother sold them."

His eyes widened, then narrowed. His voice rose as he said in astonishment, "His mother sold them?"

"Yes, sir. That's what he said."

"His mother sold them!" He said it as though he was trying to come to terms with something that was impossible to believe. I nodded. "Well," he said after a moment, "we will have to deal with this matter." He lifted the phone and asked for the police department. A physical shock ran through my chest.

"What are you going to do?" I asked in a panic. I could see him sending me away in a police car to wherever they take shoe thieves. My terror was escalating.

"Yes, Sergeant Williams. This is George Shepardson on Grove Street. I want to swear out a complaint against a Mrs. Vander on Springfield Avenue." Pause. "What's the complaint? She has stolen a pair of shoes that belong to me." Another pause. "Very well, I think we had better deal with it straightaway. I'll meet you there in a half hour. You know the place? Good." He hung up and turned to me. "You're coming with me, young man. You're going to see what kind of a mess you've created."

I was numb as I got in the car alongside my father fifteen minutes later. We drove in silence back to school and parked in front of the Vander house, waiting for the policeman to arrive.

The sergeant pulled up behind us in a black and white patrol car a moment later and got out, adjusting his hat and slipping his billy club into its holder. He had responded more quickly than he might otherwise have done, when he heard that the complainant was Colonel Shepardson. My father went to meet him. They stood behind our car for a moment discussing something, then turned toward Charlie's house. My father signaled for me to join them.

The sergeant marched up onto the porch and knocked loudly on the door. Dad stood behind him holding my hand firmly.

A woman answered the door after several knocks. I assumed it was Charlie's mother, although I couldn't guess whether she was old or young. At one point, I could see into the house. Charlie was standing in the middle of the room. He didn't seem afraid to see a policeman on his front porch. He just had a disgusted look on his face.

"Are you Mrs. Vander?" the sergeant asked.

"Yes, sir," she said in a very soft voice. She didn't seem afraid either, just tired.

"We've had a complaint sworn out against you," the officer continued.

She looked back and forth between us and the cop. "What sort of complaint?"

The sergeant looked at my father, then turned to Mrs. Vander. "This gentleman says that you sold a pair of shoes that didn't belong to you, that belonged to him."

The woman seemed to sag. She sighed deeply, then searched the policeman's face without apparent emotion. At length, she said in a voice so soft that I could barely hear her words, "Those shoes were given to my son as a gift."

My father stepped forward abruptly when he heard that, and said, "My son had no right to give those shoes to anyone. I want my shoes back, or I want the $10 I paid for them."

The sergeant put his hand on my father's arm to calm him, and said to Mrs. Vander, "Well, we have a problem here. Colonel Shepardson's boy had no right to give you those shoes, and you had no right to sell them. Now, we want to settle this matter quietly and not create a bigger problem for you or for the colonel. How much did you sell the shoes for?"

Mrs. Vander, still without any apparent emotion, said, "Two dollars."

"Two dollars!" my father exploded. "Those shoes were new and they cost me five times that much."

The cop looked at my father with some irritation. "Calm down, Colonel. We're going to get this thing settled." Turning to the woman, he said, "Do you have the two dollars?"

"No, sir," she said. "I spent it on food for my boy."

"Well, since you can't give him back the shoes, you will have to pay him $10, because that's the value of the shoes."

She looked at my father for a long moment, then said slowly, "I don't have no $10." There was silence for a moment as they all considered this impasse.

I could tell that my father was getting very angry, and I was afraid of what he was going to do next. Charlie was standing in the middle of the room listening to it all. I felt terrible about the trouble I had brought on them, and so I blurted out to my father, "I'll pay you the $10. I'll work for it and I'll pay you back."

They all looked at me, but Charlie's stare bothered me the most. I couldn't bear to see his expression. My father turned to me and said in a steely voice, "Yes, you will. You bet you will."

He shook hands with the officer, then turned without acknowledging Mrs. Vander or saying goodbye, and walked to our car. We drove home in silence while I desperately scoured my mind for ideas as to how I was going to earn the $10.

A week later, when my father came home from some kind of a meeting downtown, I could hear him talking loudly to my mother in the kitchen. He seemed to be upset. I was doing my homework in my bedroom, but his obvious excitement made me curious. I stole to the top of the stairs so I could eavesdrop on them. I was surprised when I realized that they were talking about Charlie's house. I heard him say that it had been built in 1870, and he went on about how it needed to be "raised." I didn't know how you could raise a house, but it sounded as though they were going to fix it up since it was in bad shape. However, that didn't explain why he was so upset.

I asked my mother about it the next morning, when the four of us boys were gathered at the breakfast table, and what she said shocked me. She told me that my father was trying to get the city housing authority to "raze" Charlie's house, to tear it down because of its poor condition. She explained that it was wrong to leave it standing there across from the school where all the children gathered, because it was a public health threat. And it didn't belong among the new houses that were being built around it.

It was disturbing to hear this because I felt somehow responsible. "Where will Charlie live? Does that mean he won't be coming to school with me anymore?"

"Don't worry about it," she said, trying to sooth me. "The committee refused your father's request. They're not going to force Charlie's family to move. That's why he was so upset last night."

"That's good," I said, feeling as though I had avoided causing Charlie's family a new problem. Everything had gone wrong since the moment I offered Charlie those damned shoes.

My mother explained. "A long time ago, the Vanders had a farm in that part of Springfield Avenue. Charlie's grandfather's grandfather had been born a slave, and he moved here after the Civil War when the slaves were set free. The men in his family built that house with their own hands, and they've been there for eighty years. So the people on the committee didn't want to make them move now. They've been sort of protected there all these years."

I nodded. I had known none of this before. "But why is Daddy so unhappy about it. I would think he'd be glad that Charlie doesn't have to move and leave Roosevelt School."

"Well," my mother said thoughtfully, "your father doesn't think it's healthy to leave that house there anymore. And," she added, "he's used to getting his own way."

Charlie's attendance at school became more and more uneven after that, so much so that Miss McKee stopped asking about him when he was absent. When he was present, he seemed to shrink even more deeply into himself. He sat huddled in the corner facing away from me, totally isolated from the rest of the class. I could no longer make contact with him.

Then one day, he was not only gone but his desk was cleaned out. It was as though there had never been anyone sitting in that space. I raised my hand and asked Miss McKee why Charlie's desk was empty, and she answered curtly that he had moved. She obviously didn't want to talk about it.

I was aware that I had caused Charlie's family nothing but trouble, even though I was trying to do something nice for him. I realized that they probably didn't want to see me again, but I needed to know what had happened and at least say goodbye to him. So I gathered my courage when school was over and walked around to the front of the school building, planning to cross Springfield Avenue. What I saw was such a shock that I had to sit down on the sidewalk.

Charlie's house had burned to the ground.

The chimney stood straight up on the right side of the wreckage, but the rest of the place had been reduced to blackened timber. What was left of the roof lay collapsed on top of the charred remnants of that old house. Sitting there on the cold concrete, I was so horrified that I started to cry. Everything had been so peaceful and normal before I thought of giving him my shoes. Did I cause this to happen, too?

At dinner that night, I said to no one in particular, "Charlie's house burned down."

There was an awkward silence for a moment, and then my father said, "Yes, we heard about it. Unfortunate for the family." And that was it. Subject closed.

But it wasn't closed as far as I was concerned. I needed some real closure and, since no one was going to give it to me, I was going to have to go get it for myself.

My mother often had me run errands for her after school which involved riding my bike downtown. During the week following the fire, she sent me on one of those errands and I came up with a plan. The colored section of town was on the south side of the CRRNJ tracks, only a few blocks from the store where I was going to shop. Assuming in my innocence that that's where I would find Charlie, I would ride down, look him up and see if he was okay.

With strong misgivings, I rode under the tracks and into that section of town for the first time. I'll admit that I was afraid; in fact, I was trembling all over. But I was determined to do it. The plan worked well, except that no one had ever heard of Charlie. I stopped several groups of kids and asked if they knew him, but no one did. I was about to leave, with some relief, when one older girl stopped me.

"There was a new boy in school today. I think he's living with the Grants at #248, down there on the right."

I had thought I was free to leave after proving to myself

107

that I was brave enough to go down into that neighborhood. But now I would really have to test my resolve. I turned my bike around, took a deep breath and pedaled down to #248. It was a relatively nice looking house with some flowers out front, nothing like Charlie's old place. I knocked on the door and an older lady answered.

I swallowed and asked, "Does Charlie live here?"

She looked me over, then answered, "Well, yes, he does. Who are you? Are you a friend of his?"

At that, Charlie peeked around her, then sort of jumped back in surprise. "What are you doing here?" It was almost an accusation as though he was unhappy about my appearing at his door.

"Can you come out so we can talk?" I asked.

He edged by the large lady in the door and came down onto the front stoop. He sat on the top step and asked, "Why did you come? You shouldn't be here."

"Why not?" I asked in surprise. "I came to say goodbye and to see how you were." And then I added, "And to see what happened to your house."

He snorted. In an almost angry tone, he said, "You should know."

I shook my head, baffled. "Why should I know? What happened?"

He spit out a sarcastic puff of air and said, "Someone burned us out. They set our house on fire on purpose."

I was appalled. I couldn't believe what I was hearing. It was bad enough to hear that someone had set the fire, but he was assuming that I knew something about it.

"What!" I shouted. "Who would do that? Why would they do that? I can't believe it."

He shook his head, grinning sarcastically. Very deliberately, he said, "They did it because we're black. They did it because they wanted to get us out. They did it because the town wouldn't agree to tear our house down."

I was thunderstruck. He was talking about my father. Terrible thoughts raced around in my head. The shock was so great that I didn't know what to say. Charlie helped me out. "I don't think your father set our house on fire, but I bet he knows who did." I still couldn't find the words to speak. We sat there in silence a long time.

Finally, I said, "I just wanted to say goodbye. I'll miss you."

He snorted again. "Why? You never had much to say to me. You won't even know I'm gone." Another long pause. Then he said, "It's good that you came to say goodbye. You caused my family a lot of trouble. Everything was good until you gave me those shoes."

"I know," I said. "I'm sorry. I was just trying to help."

He nodded his head. "Well," he said slowly, "thanks for coming. Goodbye." He stood up and disappeared into the house without looking back. I didn't see him again for many years.

That was 1948. I graduated from high school six years later in 1954. Reading the article in the local newspaper that listed all the high school graduates, I was looking for my name when I noticed that Charles Vander had graduated from a local Catholic high school as the class valedictorian! He was headed for Morehouse University in Atlanta. I wondered at the time where he got the money for college, since his mother didn't even have $2 to repay my dad. That was the year the Supreme Court ruled on Brown vs. Board of Education. I left for college at Rutgers in New Brunswick, New Jersey, and during my first year there, Rosa Parks made her stand – or rather, her sit-down – and from there the Civil Rights movement took off.

I was in graduate school at Temple University from 1958 to

1961, finishing up my advanced degree in criminal justice. It was one of the fields my father had agreed to pay for. After graduation, I got a job in the lab of the New Jersey State Police in Buena Vista Township. That same year, Dad died suddenly.

On a visit to my old hometown in 1965, I walked by a storefront downtown and was astonished to see emblazoned on its window the name *Charles E. Vander, Attorney at Law*. It described him as a graduate of Howard University School of Law in Washington, DC.

Going inside, I found an open room simply appointed with two desks, one of which was occupied by an attractive African-American woman. I asked if Charlie was around and she told me he was due back soon. He walked in fifteen minutes later, looked at me, did a double-take and said with a laugh, "Well, here's trouble! Mark! Are you here to cause me more problems, or because you have a problem from which only I can extricate you?"

I laughed and shook his hand. The seventeen years had done him good. He was taller and had filled out a lot, and he looked mature and self-confident. He was a far different Charlie than the one I had known, stuck in that corner of Miss McKee's 6th grade classroom.

He invited me to a tavern around the corner where we sat in a booth to catch up. Over drinks, we filled each other in on school, family and our careers. Neither of us was married yet, although we both had special women in our lives. I asked about his family and he said that both his mom and his grandfather had died, but that his sisters were living in town, which is why he set up practice here. He was now in a position to look after them. I asked what his practice consisted of, and he said he was involved in a lot of civil rights litigation and legislation.

We started to talk about the old days, and I mentioned that we were the only two in sixth grade who had straight A's.

"Yes," he said, "but you were the only one who got credit for it. Everyone else thought I was just a dumb black kid."

I shook my head. "Yeah, it must have been tough for you back then. And I didn't make things any easier for you. I always felt responsible for all the trouble you had – the cops, the fire, having to move – all of it."

He looked at me and started to laugh. I was totally mystified by what was obviously some private joke.

"What's so funny?" I finally asked. "I always felt guilty about all the trouble I caused you with those damned shoes."

He finally stopped laughing and wiped at his eyes. Still smiling broadly, he asked, "Did you know back then that I was going to college?"

"Yeah, I saw it in the paper."

He shot me an amused smile. "Did you ever wonder how a poor black kid got the money to go to college?"

I nodded. "I'll admit I wondered about it at the time. Where *did* you get the money?"

"I didn't *think* you knew," he said. "I got a couple of scholarships. But they were small compared to the $1,000 a year that I had to come up with on my own. I worked a couple of jobs while I was taking classes." He paused. "You really don't know where most of it came from?"

I looked at him and shrugged. "How would I know that?"

He stared at me for a long moment. "Well," he said, "your father paid most of my college tuition for all four years."

I just gaped at him. I was floored. *My father*? Who in the world was less likely to do such a thing? What could have possessed him to do something like that – guilt, a conversion experience, respect for Charlie's academic accomplishments, support for the civil rights movement? How could he possibly have had such a radical change of heart?

Charlie laughed as he guessed what was going through my

111

mind. "Yes," he said, "your dear old dad, rest his soul, put me through college. Without him, I would never have been where I am today."

As I tried to process this astounding information, he told me something that will stick with me for the rest of my life.

"Mark," he said, "every good thing that ever happened to me began the day you gave me those damned shoes of yours!"

VI

The Voice

My first car was a 1950 Chevrolet Styleline Two-Door Sedan. It was a crappy tan color, but I loved it. You always love your first car. I bought it in 1954 when I graduated from college and before I started graduate school. I needed it to get to class and to go see my girl.

Back then, the car cost less than $1,500 straight off the showroom floor but, since it was four years old, I paid only $650 for it. I thought I was the happiest guy in the world. My future father-in-law found it for me near the farm he owned in central Pennsylvania. I will never forget the test ride he took with me. Halfway up one of Pennsylvania's many hills, he said, "Let's see what this thing will do," and clamped his big farmer boot down over my foot on the accelerator. The car didn't actually leap up the hill, but it did make a valiant effort.

I ended up at Penn State on the main campus in State College, Pennsylvania, and was ready to begin my master's degree in engineering. I made a new friend, another engineering student, who installed the latest model radio in my car, which I had come to call Penny because of its color. The radio worked beautifully, and I found a station which played nothing but jazz and big band music. Since I was a saxophonist and had been in several bands following junior high school, I left the dial tuned there, so that the radio would blast jazz at me whenever I was in the car. My car, my radio, my music, my school – my wonderful world.

Since my girl, Ellen, was at school in Baltimore, 180 miles away, and since it took five hours to get there, I didn't make the trip very often, especially with my class schedule. She was in nursing school at Johns Hopkins Hospital and got almost *no* time off. But when we did get a chance to go somewhere together in Penny, we made sure those trips were memorable. If you know what I mean!

Mostly, we were reduced to spending a lot of money on telephone calls in the days before cell phones and calling plans. She loved jazz too, so when I had Penny's radio blasting Stan Getz or Dizzy Gillespie or Duke Ellington or Benny Goodman at me, I felt closer to her.

I was on my first trip to Baltimore before Christmas in 1954 to get Ellen and take her back to her farm for the holidays. I was getting near Harrisburg when I suddenly lost my radio signal. All I could get was static. I was spinning the dial while I drove, hoping to be able to pick up a strong Harrisburg station, but all I got was more static.

It kept getting louder and louder, and then suddenly I thought I was finding something. Underneath the noise, I could make out a man's voice. It wasn't a music program but some sort of an announcement. I strained to make it out, twisting the dial carefully. It began to come in more clearly, even though there was still quite a bit of noise in the background. When I finally understood the announcement, I straightened up in shock! What the voice had said astonished me!

Do not cross the bridge over the Susquehanna River. If you do, you will be involved in a serious traffic accident. There will be fatalities. The traffic will be tied up for three or more hours. Find an alternate route.

Then...static!

I wiggled the dial trying to get back to the station on which I had heard the announcement, but by then I had totally lost the dial position and had no idea where I had found that station. I would have given anything to hear the announcement again, just to prove to myself that I hadn't been falling asleep and imagining things. I scoured my brain, trying to remember the exact wording of the warning. Had he said there *was* an accident or that there was *going to be* an accident? He must have said that the accident had already happened, but I was sure he had said it was *going* to happen. Something like, "You *will be* in an accident," not that I would get into a traffic backup because of an accident which had already happened. "The traffic will be tied up." All the phrases were future tense. I thought the announcement started by saying not to cross the Susquehanna. But how was I supposed to get to Baltimore if I couldn't cross the river?

Ah, it was just crazy. I was hallucinating. Things like this don't happen. But I was really confused, so I stopped at a diner and got a cup of coffee. I asked the counter man if he had heard anything about an accident on the main bridge ahead, and he said no. But he assured me that they have fender benders there all the time, and they know how to handle them so as to prevent holdups. "I wouldn't worry about it, buddy," he said. "I go over it all the time, and I've never seen a traffic jam yet."

I got back in the car somewhat relieved and headed for the bridge. Turning on the radio a little suspiciously, I looked for a Harrisburg station. Nothing but static. More twirling. More static. Then...the voice. This time only the phrase *"there will be fatalities"* came through. I could barely hear it, but it let me know that I hadn't imagined it the first time. And, scariest of all, the voice sounded familiar! Was it some announcer who I had heard before, often enough to recognize? But what was he doing in Harrisburg? This was the first time I'd been here.

That was enough! I didn't go over the bridge. I stopped, pulled out my map, and looked up an alternate way to cross the river. I found another bridge downriver about ten miles, then had to work my way back onto the main road. My timidity had lost me a half hour, and I swore at myself the whole length of the detour. "You damned fool, this is a waste of time and money. What do you think you're doing? You're an engineer. You know how the universe operates. This is insanity."

When I arrived at Ellen's dorm, she was waiting in the lobby practically jumping up and down with anxiety. "Where have you been? I was so worried I was almost sick!" When I asked her why she was so upset that I was a little late, she said, "Didn't you know about it? There was a terrible accident on the Susquehanna Bridge; three people were killed. It was on the radio. It happened around the time I knew you'd be there. I was sure you were caught in the traffic jam. Or worse! The bridge is still closed."

My heart almost stopped. I had to sit down to clear my head. I couldn't say anything in response to her questions about my odd behavior, but I told her we'd go to dinner and I'd explain. We went downtown and got a special late edition of the *Baltimore Sun.* The front page was covered with photos of a massive traffic jam, and shots of several cars in a tangled wreckage. Two men and a woman had been killed, and five more people were seriously injured. I read every detail twice, then looked at Ellen with total mystification and shock.

"How did you avoid seeing that mess?" she asked. "You had to be coming that way. I was sure you'd get caught in it. I was afraid you were one of the people who were...injured."

After a while, I shook my head and quietly said, "I didn't go that way." A long pause. Then I looked her in the eye and said, "I was...warned."

Ellen was a practical no-nonsense type who thought rationally. She wanted to be a nurse because she was interested in science and in technical knowledge. She studied constantly which had always put her at the head of her class. My interest in music and art was not what attracted her to me, but rather my desire to become an engineer. I knew that what I was going to tell her would not go over well. Neither of us was religious; we didn't believe in magic or miracles. Or God, for that matter. Spirituality wasn't scientific. It was not something you could prove.

On the one hand, I wanted to tell her the truth, partly because I wanted to hear myself describe what had happened. That way I might be able to believe it myself. On the other hand, I was reluctant to tell her, not only because she wouldn't believe me, but because it was so personal and extraordinary that I didn't want her making fun of me or dismissing it as my imagination. I was having a hard time deciding how to proceed.

"What do you mean you were warned?" she asked. "Were there signs up to avoid the bridge?"

I thought about it. "Sort of."

She was frowning. "You're acting funny about this. Just tell me how you avoided the bridge. I was so worried. I want to know how you escaped that mess. How were you warned?"

"It was something on the radio," I said finally.

She nodded. "So, there was an announcement after it happened that warned you away from the bridge." I studied her face. She gave me a frustrated look. "That was it, wasn't it?" Pause. "Why not just say so?"

"Because it wasn't...quite like that."

She was getting upset. "What is the matter with you? Why not just give me a straight answer?"

"Because you won't like the answer." I said it too loudly

117

and people looked over at our table.

She was silent for a long time, and I recognized her angry mood. In a very tense voice, she said, "It's a simple question. Why not a simple answer?"

"All right," I said. "I'll tell you, and then we'll drop it." I took a deep breath. "There was static on the radio as I got near to Harrisburg. Then a voice came on the radio and said, 'Don't go on the bridge. There's going to be an accident and people are going to be killed.'"

She looked at me quizzically, and then tried to suppress a laugh. "Do you know how dumb that sounds? I thought you were trying to hide something, like a woman in the backseat. What really happened?"

"That's what happened," I said. "I told you that you weren't going to like it."

She smoothed the napkin in her lap, took a drink, and gave me an amused look. "You're telling me you were warned about the accident...before it happened?

I nodded for a while. "Yup."

She fooled with her napkin some more, folded it carefully and threw it on the table, then said, "Well, if you don't want to tell me, I'm not going to pick a fight over it. I just don't know why you're acting this way."

I said, "I can only tell you what happened. Anyway, the real issue is I'm OK and I avoided the trouble. Let's leave it at that."

And that was the last we said about it. I did write it up later and kept it in the back of one of my school notebooks but, after a while, when I came across it, I would feel stupid and consider tearing it up. But I didn't.

Ellen and I were married three years later, when I was out of grad school and she had her R.N. degree. We moved to New Jersey where I went to work for the Jersey Central Power and

Light in Elizabeth, and she got a job in the ER in a small hospital in Westfield where we lived. We were very happy and, when she got pregnant in 1959, we looked forward to expanding our family. She continued to work until two weeks before her due date. She was healthy and felt fine, except for the normal discomfort at that point in a pregnancy.

I was supposed to attend a two-day meeting in Trenton which meant that I would have to stay overnight, since the sessions lasted well into the evening. I was reluctant to be so far away and leave her alone for so long, but my boss was not moved by my situation. So I said goodbye to Ellen in the morning, asked her again if she was going to be okay, and was assured that she had lots of resources to call on. We had good neighbors, her sister lived half an hour away, and her doctor was a personal friend. The hospital was nearby and was filled with work associates who knew of her condition. So she waved me off, telling me she was no longer a little girl. I patted her belly and told her that I had noticed that fact!

We had long since traded Penny for a 1958 Pontiac Super Chief 4-Door Sedan, and I made certain that it contained a good radio. If I thought about my experience with the voice on the radio, which I seldom did, I felt that it was somehow associated with that other radio in Penny. So, to my mind, that had been a freak occurrence which would never happen again.

I had just settled in for the hour-long drive and was about ten miles from home. I was listening to *In the Mood,* my favorite Glenn Miller number, when the program went off the air and was replaced by static. A cold shiver went up my spine because I was instantly back in Harrisburg, closing in on the Susquehanna Bridge. I twisted the dial, trying to get back to Glenn Miller, when the familiar voice surfaced from under the static. It said: *"Return home. Now!"*

This time I didn't question it. I made a U-turn, broke the

speed limit all the way home, and burst into the house. Ellen was sitting on the living room sofa reading a magazine. She almost jumped out of her skin when I slammed the door open. She looked at me in confusion and asked, "What's wrong? What are you doing here?" Then she got an impish expression on her face, and said, "I know, you wanted to catch me with my boyfriend."

I didn't laugh. "Are you OK?" I asked.

She made a face as if I was asking a dumb question. "Well, I'm still here. I feel fine. What would make you come back?"

I wasn't going to get into that right then. "I had the feeling you needed me. But I guess I was just being a worry wart. This is our first baby, and we're both a little tense."

I went to the sofa and kissed her on the forehead, then said, "I'm going to call the office and tell them I'm not going to be at the conference. My assistant can stand in for me."

She gave me a funny look and got up to come with me as I turned and started for the study. That's when I heard the thump of her body hitting the floor. I rushed to her and lifted her head, but she was unconscious and I could see blood on the front of her nightgown. In a panic, I called both the ambulance and the hospital, and in no time she was in the same ER in which she worked. A number of her friends made her priority-one. I didn't even have time to say goodbye to her, because she was rushed to the OR where they delivered the baby by C-section and performed a hysterectomy.

Dr. Evanston, her gynecologist, came in and sat down with me in the waiting room an hour later. Wearily shoving his scrub cap back off his head, he sighed and said, "Well, that was as near a thing as I ever want to see. If the ambulance had been five minutes later, you could have lost both of them."

I was having a hard time focusing on what he was saying. "Is she OK?" I asked anxiously.

"Yes, she'll be fine, but she won't be caring for your daughter for a few days."

I broke in. "It's a girl? Is she OK?"

"She's perfect. She's beautiful. They're both good. You don't have anything to worry about. I'm just glad you got them here in time."

"So am I," I said, my head spinning. I couldn't believe what had happened. I got up and went in to see Ellen who was so drugged that she could barely open her eyes.

"How's the baby?" she murmured. I assured her she was okay. She turned to me, her eyes closed, and whispered, "I'm glad you came home."

I squeezed her hand and said, "So am I."

It wasn't until two weeks later when we were back home with our new baby, Josie Marie, that Ellen brought it up again. "Just why did you come back home? I was fine when you left, and your boss didn't want you to miss the conference."

I paused, staring at her and picking my words carefully. "I got a...feeling that you might need me."

She scowled, trying to figure out what I meant. "What kind of a feeling? Are you psychic or something?"

I took a deep breath and sighed. "I might as well tell you," I said, dreading her response. "Do you remember that Christmas when I was coming to get you in Baltimore and there was that terrible crash on the Susquehanna Bridge?"

"Yeah."

"Do you remember...?"

She cut me off. "Your car radio?" I nodded. "You're going to tell me it was your car radio again?"

"I can't help it," I said. "That's what happened. Static when I should have been getting a strong signal. And then a man's voice with three words – 'Return home now!' So I did a U-turn and got home in time to be here when you collapsed."

She studied my face for a long time. "How is that possible?"

"How? Why not ask me who the guy on the radio is? I don't know that either." I almost laughed. "Somebody lives in my radio and alerts me when there's some kind of danger. The voice sounds vaguely familiar, but I can't figure out who it is or where it's coming from."

She shook her head. "Things like this can't happen. It's like a warning about the future before it occurs."

I shrugged. "I don't understand it. But it's worked twice now. Are we going to pretend it didn't happen just because we don't understand what's going on?"

We both sat in silence for a while, pondering the mystery. Then she said, "Well, whatever it was, it saved my life." Then she added, "And Josie's, too."

The voice never gave me a warning when anyone else was in the car. So no one else ever heard it, which made it harder to convince people that the "messages" were more than just lucky guesses on my part. It happened three more times in the next ten years, which eventually made Ellen a believer.

The first told me about lightning damage to the house wiring which could have caused a fire. The electrician confirmed this warning. Another was about a certain day when a rabid dog would be in the neighborhood, at a time when Josie was five and was spending much of her time outdoors. The dog was shot by a cop who happened to be passing. The third one warned me about a furnace repairman who would have checked out our house and then returned with his pals to tie us up and ransack the place. He was later arrested for doing the same thing in a neighbor's home. In each case, the voice warned us of a danger that could have seriously injured one or more of us. After the fifth message, Ellen had no more doubts about our peculiar phenomenon.

There was one incident that confused me, though, one serious problem that the voice did *not* warn me against. And I have always wondered why that was. I was rear-ended one day by a speeding driver on one of the narrow two-lane bridges in Elizabeth, and shoved into the car ahead of me. The three of us were jammed together for an hour. An ambulance went by us in the opposite direction right after it happened with its siren screaming, but that was the last vehicle across the bridge, because traffic was halted while the emergency squads tried to sort things out. I wish I had had a warning to avoid the bridge that day, but it didn't come. I wondered if the voice might have decided to take a vacation around that time.

So it was that when the final message came through the radio years later, when Josie was eighteen and almost through her senior year in high school, Ellen and I paid special attention to it. I reported the voice's words to Ellen as accurately as I could. The static prelude had become a warning, so it helped me concentrate on the message and remember it precisely. This is the warning I repeated to Ellen:

Josie's prom date is not trustworthy. He will get drunk, will drug Josie, and will assault her. She must not be allowed to go to the prom with him.

Ellen listened in open-mouthed horror. "What are we going to do?" she asked me. "How can we possibly handle this? She'll never believe us."

And she was right. We sat down with Josie a day later and tried to have a serious conversation about this warning. Josie had heard us talking over the years about the voice in the radio, but she had always treated it as a joke. We reminded her of the previous five messages and how they had all proven true, preventing injury to one or more of us. But she looked at us in amazement. "You want me to miss my senior prom because of a mysterious voice on the radio? You've got to be *kidding*!"

We worked on her for days, but she wouldn't take the warning seriously. We threatened to not let her go at all, but she responded that she was already eighteen and we couldn't stop her. We finally reached a compromise when she agreed to go with a group of stag girls and meet her date at the dance, promising never to be alone with him. I even called one of the faculty chaperones whom I happened to know well, and told her that we had reason to suspect that Josie's date was untrustworthy, and that he might be a threat to her if he got drunk. The advisor assured us that there would be no drinking, and that the boy in question was one of the star members of the football team and a model student in the senior class. We were uneasy about the whole thing, but it was 1977, Josie was eighteen and headed for college, and there wasn't a whole lot we could do about it short of locking her up.

The girls all gathered at our house because Josie was one of the most popular members of the class, and the rest of them were thrilled to be in her group. We admired their dresses, took pictures, saw them off in several cars, and then sat down to pray that they would have a happy – and safe – prom experience.

The prom was to end at midnight, after which the girls were gathering at one of their homes for an after-prom party and sleepover. *Sans* boys, of course. We went to bed about 1:00 after having held our joint breaths for several hours. I slept lightly and was awake when the phone rang about 4:00. It was one of Ellen's work associates at the hospital informing us that Josie had been admitted. We rushed to the ER and found her in one of the examining rooms. She was still in her prom dress which was torn and soiled. One of her friends was sitting by her side, holding her hand. Josie's face was streaked with tears, and she burst into violent sobs when she saw us.

We hugged her and asked her what had happened. Her friend told us what Josie was unable to, that some of the guys had crashed the party, that the boy who was supposed to have been Josie's date had enticed her into his car, had drugged and assaulted her, and then had dropped her off back at the girl's house. We were interrupted by the doctor who came to perform an examination for forensic purposes.

The next few days were a nightmare. Josie stayed in the hospital overnight, then spent a week in her room out of touch with everyone. Friends brought her homework, but she wasn't motivated to do anything. She came down for dinner but rarely said two words; she ate the rest of her meals in her room. We began to worry about her sanity. The school was very accommodating since she was an honors student, but this couldn't go on forever, especially at the end of her senior year with an acceptance for the fall term at the University of Virginia.

Then one night a week later, she came down to dinner and announced that it was over and she was ready to go back to school. She looked at us with tear-filled eyes and said, "I thought you guys were crazy to take that radio thing seriously. But I should have listened to you. I knew it had told the truth in the past, but I just wanted to go to the prom so badly." She started to cry, so we both got up and hugged her. She recovered quickly in the following days, testified at the trial of the boy who had attacked her, and regained her energy as she started to get ready to go off to college.

That was the last time I ever heard the voice. I didn't know whether we lived more carefully after that, or whether the voice had simply gotten tired of running interference for us. But that whole mystery gradually faded into a foggy past and made us wonder as we got into our 80's whether it had all really happened.

And then…

I found myself here. I don't remember dying. I do recall being sick for a long time and having Ellen by my side acting as my private nurse. But then, when I opened my eyes once, I was here. And it startled the hell out of me. It was the biggest shock of my life. As you know, it took me a long time to accept the fact that I was still alive even though I was dead! Someone should have told me about this. Well, I guess they tried, but I wasn't listening.

Anyway, as you know, I was assigned work to do. I had no idea that there was a place like this, and was even more surprised to discover that we still have to work on this side of reality. It was made clear to me that I was assigned my particular job specifically because I hadn't believed all this spiritual guardian angel stuff while I was still on Earth.

You assigned me to watch over and protect my former self. I could see the man I used to be, in my familiar but recently vacated body, but I had no sense of ownership or identity with him. He was like a stranger to me, so I can refer to him only as "he," not as "me." Yet the aura of total love in this place made me care for him deeply, and so I did my best to fulfill my responsibilities.

I was given a list of the things that he had agreed to accomplish while on Earth. But there was also a second list – all the things which might threaten his safety and interfere with the completion of his goals. It was my job to see that those problems were dealt with, so that he could succeed and not die before the proper time.

I was able to see, as though on an immense television screen, what his family was doing at any given moment. I had to decide when, or even whether, to intervene so as to protect them all. It was essential that they complete their various missions.

I studied the papers – both his goals and all the possible problems that might intervene – and set to work. Immediately, I sensed a threat. He was driving toward Baltimore, totally oblivious of the danger ahead of him. I focused my energy as I had been instructed to do, picking my words carefully so that my thoughts could get through to him. I said:

Do not cross the bridge over the Susquehanna River. If you do, you will be involved in a serious traffic accident. There will be fatalities. The traffic will be tied up for three or more hours. Find an alternate route.

But I also had to use my discretion as to when *not* to interfere with events on Earth. On one occasion, I could see a problem looming before him as he approached a narrow two-lane bridge in Elizabeth. There was going to be an accident in which he would be involved. I could have removed him from the scene. But I also knew that the cause of the accident would be a drunk driver behind him who was speeding recklessly. I realized that his wife, Ellen, was on duty caring for a patient in an ambulance heading across that same bridge from the opposite direction. If I had kept him off the bridge that day, the drunk driver would have crossed over and crashed head-on into Ellen's speeding ambulance.

The Lighter

He was grumbling as he drove the detour for what felt like the hundredth time. A bridge was out on the main road into town. They had been rebuilding it for eight months, and he lived on the wrong side of the construction. The only route into town now was by way of a five-mile detour that added fifteen minutes to his commute. He resented every foot of the way, since that long detour was required to get around only fifty yards of closed road. When were they ever going to open the thing? Everyone in his end of town was up in arms about it. Whenever they passed close to the new bridge, no one seemed to be working. It just sat there looking like it was finished, but guarded by enormous barriers that screamed *"BRIDGE CLOSED – USE DETOUR →"*

Because Henry was a solo dentist, he couldn't just take a day off once in a while to avoid the inconvenience. He had staff whose salaries he had to pay along with other office expenses, and patients with whom he had to keep on good terms. But every time he drove that blasted detour, his resentment grew. Somebody ought to get sacked for their poor management and planning.

His three kids, on the other hand, got a kick out of the new way home, as they called it. It went through farm country, and they mashed their faces up against the car windows to see how many cows they could count, how many colts they could see running through the paddocks, how many tractors they could identify by color and size. It was a game to them, but Henry was sick of hearing them moo out the windows when they drove by the pastures. The kids held contests to see how many cows would turn their heads to look at them, wondering if there might be a sister bovine in the car. Jack usually won; at eleven, he was the eldest one of the trio. Brayden was nine, a quiet boy who preferred to read books rather than get his clothes soiled. RJ was the wild one of the bunch, spurred into constant noisy activity by trying to keep up with his older brothers. He was five.

Henry was forty. He and Angie were married while he was still in dental school, and had become parents two years after he had set up practice in a little town in Ohio. He picked the location, thirty miles north of Columbus, specifically because there was no other dentist there. The population of about a thousand had taken to him immediately, and his practice had flourished from the start, drawing people from twenty miles around. Angie, who stayed home with the kids, had been trained as a dental assistant and helped out in the office when she was needed. If she resented not being paid, she was compensated by enjoying the little extras they could afford because of Henry's not having to pay another employee.

Henry was an only child, and his mother lived in Cleveland, refusing to move closer to his family. She was sixty, was actively involved in Republican politics there, and didn't want to trade that life for one of uncompensated babysitting. Her husband had been killed in combat in Germany during 1944 when Henry was twelve, and his death had left a permanent scar on the family. There had been no opportunities for goodbyes and final loving words. He had been overseas since 1942 and, when the war ended, he simply hadn't come home. There was no sealed casket, no officer bearing personal belongings, merely a letter expressing the regrets of the war department. Henry, ten years old at the time his father shipped out, missed him desperately. They had been very close, playing sports together and taking in a variety of ballgames on weekends. Henry's father, James, was a big man, and had been a foreman in a construction company. Henry thought his father could do anything, and loved squeezing his enormous biceps. He felt safe as long as his father was around, so the thought of his leaving was a scary one. As James prepared to ship out in 1942, Henry saved up money to buy him a goodbye gift, a Zippo lighter. He spent $2.00 for it, along with another $1.00 to have it engraved with his father's initials – JKS for James Knox Shilling. Then, secretly, Henry had scratched his own initial "H" on the bottom of the lighter. James was very touched by the gift, because he was a heavy smoker and it would be a constant reminder of the son he had left at home, a son fortunately young enough to escape the draft.

Henry felt a tremendous surge of pride when he presented the lighter to his father, and often imagined him using it in his foxholes in France and Germany. Sadly, though, his father had been gone for three years by the time the war ended, and Henry had grown so accustomed to his absence that the news of his death did not seem real, and had no lasting emotional impact on him. His father took on the aura of a mystical hero who had gone off to fight Hitler and who had been killed in the process. Henry imagined a variety of scenarios that had caused his death, all of them heroic.

Henry's mother had never gotten over her anger at the impersonal way in which the army had handled the matter. They told her that he had been killed in action in 1944, but she never got word of it until 1945 when the war was almost over. Her anger had taken her into local and then county politics. She had helped a friend get elected county controller, after which she had been given a supervisory job in the office. But she wore her widowhood like a badge of honor, and never let anyone forget what a sacrifice her husband had made. No one was more patriotic than she, and she waved the flag on every possible occasion.

Henry had little time for politics or anything other than his practice and his three sons. He was an exemplary father and was always taking the kids somewhere exciting, so that they cherished their time with him. He never forgot how much of his younger life had been spent without a father.

Fortunately, the boys were not in the backseat this day in 1972. He was returning from a ten-hour session in the office, and his back hurt more than usual. One hostile kid had bitten him on his left pinky finger and he was still feeling the pain. He was exhausted and could think only of sitting down with a drink before dinner. The detour was such a habit that he could drive it with his eyes closed, which was almost the case at this moment.

Up ahead was a right turn that most of the traffic took to remain on the shortest leg of the detour. You could see a line of cars during rush hour approaching this intersection, all of them with their right turn signals blinking. He always turned right there too, but this night he had promised Angie he would get bananas for the kids. They were always out of bananas. To stop at the mini-mart meant passing that side road and driving straight ahead another half mile. He was some distance back from the line of cars turning right, so when they cleared the way, he gunned the engine, thinking only of making his purchase and getting home.

The woman in the gray Honda, sitting on that side road waiting to pull out into the intersection, assumed that Henry was going to turn right like everyone else. So she started her left turn just as Henry sailed past. He hit her car directly on the driver's door, shoving the car sideways twenty feet past the intersection. The noise of the impact was horrendous. When the cars came to a stop, Henry was dazed but conscious. Because air bags were not yet standard, he was thrown into the steering column and the windshield in spite of wearing his seat belt. He was bleeding from the face and scalp when several people rushed up to pull him from his wrecked car. They laid him on the grass beside the road, while a nearby homeowner called for an ambulance.

The woman in the other car was another matter. She was pinned in the driver's seat by the front end of Henry's car. The door had collapsed on top of her, and she was trapped between the crushed side of the car and the passenger's seat. She was bleeding profusely and appeared to be unconscious. Passersby attempted to reach her from the other side of the car, but were afraid to try moving her.

It took the emergency squad and the wreckers an hour to get her stabilized, to clear the area, and to transport both of them to the hospital. Henry had a concussion, a broken nose, and lacerations of his scalp and forehead. He spent a night in the hospital before being released. Angie and the kids visited him that evening, and were relieved to find him in great good humor, in spite of a black eye, a swollen nose, and bandages on his head. Brayden thought he looked like a monster in a nightmare. That amused everyone.

Henry was discharged the next morning and told to take a week to recover. Before he left the hospital, he tried to see the woman who had caused the accident, but was told she was still in a coma. When he asked about her relatives, the nurse said she had no family members in the country.

Henry rested for four days before the inactivity began to get to him. So he called his office manager and told her to get things cranked up for work the following day. He went back to the office with an eye that was still black, a nose that was still broken, and a headache that wouldn't go away, but work was therapeutic and he began to feel better when the patients arrived. They were all very concerned about him, and didn't seem to mind having a monster from a nightmare fiddling around in their mouths.

But in the back of his mind, the woman from the accident kept bothering him. He wondered how she was doing because, when he was honest about it, he had to admit that he felt a little guilty, just slightly responsible for what had happened. He remembered gunning the motor when the last car cleared the intersection, in his hurry to get home. If he hadn't sped up, could he have stopped in time to prevent the accident?

He went back to the hospital a week later and asked for her room number. Standing in the doorway, he could see that she was conscious. He rapped on the door to attract her attention, and she turned in his direction. "Do you feel like a short visit?" he asked. She scowled slightly, as if trying to figure out who he was. Or perhaps it was just a reaction to his still bruised face and the dressing on his forehead. Then she nodded.

He stood by her bed and said, "You can see from my looks that I was in an accident." He waited a moment, then added, "It was the same one you were in."

Her eyes opened wider in comprehension. She reached for his hand and said, "I'm so sorry. I am told it was my fault. But I don't remember any of it." She had kind eyes, but was obviously in a lot of pain. And she had a rather strong German accent.

"How are you getting along?" he asked.

She moved as if to relieve her painful position. "I have a broken hip and some broken ribs and lots of bruises. But I'm tough and I will live." She spoke slowly with the hesitation of someone who was tired and feeling ill.

"Well," he said, "I just wanted to say hello and see how you were doing. I hope you recover quickly. Can I stop again when you're feeling better?"

She nodded. "I don't want to talk too much now because I lost some teeth. So I look ugly."

He laughed. "Well, for one thing, you don't look ugly. And for another, I'm a dentist. So maybe we can talk some time about your missing teeth."

She smiled in spite of herself, inadvertently showing him the extent of her injury – missing upper left medial and lateral incisors. That would definitely have to be fixed. She was an attractive woman whom he guessed to be in her late 40's or perhaps 50. The missing teeth would detract seriously from her appearance.

"That would be nice," she murmured, responding to his implication about fixing her teeth. "I don't want to look like a war refugee." That German accent. It made him wonder.

He said goodbye and started to leave, then turned back and added, "I'm Doctor Henry Shilling. I'll drop in again sometime."

She reached out to shake his hand. "I'm Gerda Lehmann."

He nodded and said, "It's nice to meet you. But I'm sorry it had to be this way." She grinned again, then covered her mouth self-consciously. He smiled. "We'll talk about fixing that when everything else is all healed up."

Two months later he checked to see if she was listed in the local phone directory. Her name was there alongside an address in the nearby suburb of Gahanna, about ten miles away. He called and was surprised when she answered immediately. "Helloo?" That funny European inflection.

"Hello, Gerda? This is Doctor Shilling. You know, the guy who ran into you with his car. I called to see how your recovery is coming along."

"Oh, hello, Doctor. I'm doing fine, thank you. I'm taking rehab for my hip, and my broken ribs are much better."

"I wondered if I could come by to see you. We have some things to discuss." Gerda said yes, so he found himself in her living room on the following Saturday afternoon. He started off by telling her that, though his lawyer was urging him to sue her for damages and liability, he wasn't going to do so. His insurance had paid his hospital bills and replaced his car. He knew that she had been charged with negligence and would probably face a stiff fine, and he felt that that was sufficient punishment. He also noted that she was still unable to walk because of her fractured hip, so he had no desire to make her life any more difficult.

"Have you talked to anyone about replacing your missing teeth?" he asked, after they had chatted for a while.

She shook her head. "I don't have the money to do that for awhile. The court costs are going to use up a lot of what I have, and I can't take on any other expenses right now."

He smiled at her, "I may be able to help with that. When you're able to walk, I'd like to do a restoration for you. I can build you a bridge that will look just like your regular teeth."

"Oh," she said, shaking her head, "that's very nice. But I could never afford that."

"No charge," he assured her. "The dentist knocked your teeth out, and I think the dentist should replace them. Don't you agree?"

Her eyes widened in surprise. "You would do that?"

"Absolutely! It's the kind of thing I do all the time. I think you've suffered enough. This might take some of the sting out of your recovery."

A month later, he was back for another visit. By then she was walking with the help of a cane, which she had been told she would never be able to do without. The accident had permanently injured her hip.

They got to talking and she told him something about herself. Born in Germany, she had lived there through the Second World War. She had been in Frankfurt when the Third US Army had overrun it.

"Really?" he asked, surprised. "My father was with the 87th Infantry Division, part of the Third Army. They called them the Golden Acorn."

She had remained in the city until 1950. At that time, she and her five-year-old son had moved to Bonn to be near the west, since she was hoping to move to the United States. But money and the difficulty of obtaining a visa had frustrated her for years. The authorities were punishing her because of her work for the Nazis. By the time she was able to get her visa in 1965, her son was already twenty and had a good paying job with Merck Darmstadt, the huge chemical and pharmaceutical company.

"So, you came over by yourself?" She nodded. "What about your husband?"

She searched his eyes cautiously. "I've never been married."

He waited a moment, then said, "Oh, I see. And why did you decide to leave Germany?"

She thought for a long time. "There are more opportunities here. I'm still not comfortable with the climate over there. My father was a Jew and I barely escaped the concentration camps." She struggled with her memories for awhile. "I worked for the Nazis before the war began, and they were so used to me that I got overlooked." She was silent again for a while, then added, "And my son's father was from America."

Henry nodded. "So he was a soldier?"

"Yes, I met him when he was stationed in Frankfurt. I was

only twenty and he could get me food and clothing. We only met a few times, but we were truly in love. I tried to write him after he left Frankfurt, but I never heard from him again."

"And you're here trying to find him?"

"Oh, no, he was killed in 1945. He had told them to send his belongings to me in case something happened, so I received a parcel and a letter from his captain. But there was no note from him. I don't think he ever knew he had a son."

Several weeks later, Gerda came to the office to begin her restoration work. They had become quite good friends by then, and Henry continued to be concerned about her progress. He made a series of appointments for her and, by six months after the accident, she had been fitted with her new bridge, and her recovery seemed complete, except for her limp and the cane.

The day after she received her new bridgework, she called the office to report that she had lost her cigarette lighter somewhere, and wondered if she might have left it in the waiting room. Henry's assistant searched the cushions on the sofa and found it. She laid it on the counter in the inner office by the telephone in preparation for calling Gerda.

That was where Henry first saw it.

It was a battered Zippo lighter, the stainless steel case stained nevertheless, showing the evidence of hard usage. Henry couldn't remember seeing another Zippo since he had presented his father with his gift twenty-eight years before. Curious, he picked it up. And froze in shock!

It bore the engraved initials "JKS."

He held it in his hand for a long moment, half afraid to turn it over. When he finally managed to do so, he could see the letter "H" still faintly visible where he had scratched it with his penknife almost three decades earlier.

Lightheaded, he leaned back against the counter to keep from falling. His office manager saw the expression on his face and asked if he was all right. All he could do was nod.

She said, "I was going to call Gerda and tell her we found her lighter."

Waving her off, he said, "That's all right. I'll do it myself. I...have to go see her."

He arranged for a meeting, not knowing if he was angry or merely curious. Mostly he was confused. He had no idea now what to think of her.

He sat on her sofa and handed her the lighter without a word. She took it, examined it in her palm for a moment, then said, "Thank you for finding it."

He looked her in the eye for the first time. Then it occurred to him – "You meant for me to find it, didn't you?"

Her face clouded over. "I've been wanting to talk to you about this, to tell you the truth, for a long time. But now that the moment is here, I'm afraid you're going to want to reject me."

There was a tense silence on both sides. "So you did something that should make me want to reject you?" No response. "Well, you can start by telling me where you got this lighter."

"I already told you. The army sent it to me along with the rest of Jim's...uh, your father's things."

"So," he said, shaking his head in disbelief, "you're telling me that your lover was my father?" She nodded. He stared at her, open-mouthed, trying to process this incredible information. Then, recovering, he asked, "Why did he have his things sent to you instead of sending them back to us?"

"Because," she said, shaking her head slowly, "he didn't plan to go back home."

Henry scowled at her in disbelief. "What the hell would make you say something like that?"

She was visibly trembling. He knew that this was difficult

for her, but he wasn't inclined to make it any easier. She continued, "I said we were only together a few times, but we spent all that time talking. It was like he was desperate for someone to talk to, because he was badly confused about what he wanted to do in the future. He knew the war was going to end soon, and he wasn't sure he wanted to go back to his life before the war. He loved you very much and talked about you a lot, but I think if he had returned he would have divorced your mother. The war had changed a lot of things about the way he thought."

"Wait a minute!" Henry yelled. "Are you telling me that he was the father of your son?"

She searched his face carefully, then nodded.

"Oh, God!" he muttered, sinking back into the sofa. He put his head in his hands for a moment, trying to sort through his feelings. "How do I know that's true? It could have been any soldier."

She didn't react to the insult. "No," she said, almost whispering. "It could only have been him. I wasn't a prostitute. There was no one else. I loved him."

"Do you have any other good news for me, or is that it?" he growled.

She shook her head. "Are you sure you want to hear it all right now?"

He stared at her with an exasperated expression. "Well, go ahead. What can be worse than that?"

She took her time. Eventually, she said in a very quiet voice, "He didn't die in 1944. And he wasn't killed in action."

"Shit!" He almost yelled it. Everything that he had believed was being yanked out from under him. He felt as though he were floating in space with no place to land. Unable to handle any more, he got up, slammed out the front door and sped home.

That night, after the boys were in bed, Angie and he had a long conversation with a lot of tears. When they were both emotionally exhausted, there were still questions to be answered. Lots of them.

Why had she come here? Did she know who he was before she came? What did she want? What should they tell his mother? What about the half-brother? On and on. The implications were overwhelming. He knew he would have to confront her again, but he kept postponing the call. She solved the problem by calling him.

"Well," he said on the phone, "I left so fast last time that I forgot to take the lighter with me. I really want to keep it." They made a date and Angie went with him this time.

With the introductions made and the awkward small talk behind them, Henry said, "You told me that he wasn't killed in combat. Suppose you tell me what *did* happen."

"I hate to tell you this because it causes me pain, too," she said. "He was killed at Darmstadt after the city was taken in March 1945. But he died in an auto accident." Pause. "He was driving. And he was drunk." Another pause. "And there was a German woman in the car who was also killed. I don't know who she was, but that's why they covered it up and told you he was killed in combat in 1944. That's in the official record. But the soldier who delivered his things to me told me the truth."

Henry just sat there shaking his head as Angie put her arm around his shoulder. "How much worse can it get?" he moaned.

"That's the whole story," Gerda hurried to add. "No more surprises. No more sad news."

They all sat thinking for a while. Then he sat up, squared himself and took a deep breath. "OK, now let's figure out why you're here and what you want. I suppose you're looking for money."

"No! No money," she said hurriedly.

"Well, you obviously want something or you wouldn't be here. Why don't you just tell us that whole side of the story, too?"

She leaned toward them. "I'm a woman alone," she began. "I have no family here or in Germany, other than my son. Many of them were killed in the Holocaust. There was no future for me in Germany, but my son refused to leave. I came ahead, partly to get established here in hopes that he would someday choose to join me. Also, I hoped to contact your family. I didn't know how that would happen, but I thought you might want to meet Kurt. Or at lease know of his existence. And I thought you might be able to help him get his visa. It would be easier if we had someone here who would vouch for him."

She sat back as if drained from finally having put these thoughts into words. She glanced at them to judge their reaction. It was Angie who spoke next. "Why is he reluctant to come to the U.S.?"

"Because he's heard too many bad reports from friends who have come here, how they've been greeted with hostility for having fought on the other side."

"But surely he was too young to have fought."

"People don't take that into account. He's a German, and Germans killed their father or their son or someone they knew. Anyone with a German accent is suspect."

"How sad," Angie whispered.

Henry felt anger rising in his chest. "So this whole thing was a set-up. You came here so you could just accidentally stumble across us, and then you just accidentally left your lighter in my office."

"Well," she said with the hint of a smile, showing off her new bridge, "I didn't know how easy you were going to make it for us to meet. I didn't plan that part of it. I mean, I didn't pull out in front of you knowing that it was you. I think providence planned that part of the story."

"How did you know where to find me after all these years?"

She nodded and showed them the note which his father's captain had sent along with his personal items. It contained James' last known address as well as the names of his wife and son. Some of his papers also indicated that he lived in the Cleveland area. She concluded by saying, "A little detective work was all that was needed after that." Then, sensing that they still had unanswered questions, she went on. "I've been here since 1966. I didn't want anything from you, except maybe a little help in getting Kurt over here. So I was going to wait until he was ready and then see about contacting you."

They struggled through another half hour of details, then got up to leave. "We're going to have to do a lot of talking with family," Henry told her.

The next weekend, Henry and his family drove up to Cleveland to visit his mother. While the kids played with neighbor children, he told his mother the whole story. She was, not surprisingly, outraged by the idea and refused to believe any of it. "She's one of those women who turned to whoring after the war to survive. You can't trust a thing she says."

"You don't want to look into the matter of the son, in case what she says is true, and he is Dad's...son?"

"Why would I want to do that?" she exploded. "He is *not* your dad's son. And even if he were, why would I want to see him. He's a total stranger, and he's the bastard child of..." And she stormed out of the room.

Angie and Henry seemed able to talk about the situation calmly and thoughtfully in the following weeks. And as time went on, they came to a place of acceptance about the possibility of Kurt's coming here and being a small part of their lives. It might be nice for the kids to have an uncle, even half of an uncle, since Angie only had one sister.

"But you know," Angie reminded him, "if you do anything like this, you'll probably lose touch with your mother. I hope she'll relent, but you know how she is."

So Henry called Gerda and said they were ready to talk. She replied, "Oh, I'm so happy you called. I've been praying that you would. Kurt is thinking about coming here to be near me because he just got engaged. He's talking about bringing his fiancée with him so we can be a family, especially if there are children."

The next months were spent in research into the steps that had to be taken. But their plans were complicated by a sudden and unexpected decline in Henry's health. His symptoms seemed to puzzle his doctors – loss of appetite, lethargy, fatigue, increasingly higher blood pressure. Even though they treated the symptoms, he got steadily worse. By the time he had started taking days off from work, his doctor finally suggested a specialist who did a thorough workup. What he discovered was alarming in the extreme – Henry had an advanced case of renal failure. If it was allowed to proceed untreated much longer, he could die.

All this time, Henry had been fulfilling his promises to Gerda, and had made arrangements to have Kurt and his fiancée, Kirsten, come to Ohio. They would stay with Gerda until they had time to find a place of their own, after the wedding. Both of them were very excited. They had been tentatively promised jobs at one of the Columbus hospitals, Kurt as a lab assistant and Kirsten as a nurse's aide, until she could study for and take her nursing boards. Thus, a year after the accident, Gerda was preparing to reunite her family in her new country.

By then, however, Henry had given up his practice. He was undergoing dialysis three times a week, but was not showing the improvement they had hoped for. Everyone was worried about his prospects, and the best medical opinion was that only a kidney transplant would save his life. Since this procedure was relatively new, there was no comprehensive database for live donors, so finding a kidney was primarily a matter of advertising the need through media and by word of mouth.

Kurt and Kirsten were married in Gahanna, Ohio, Gerda's home, in June, and began work at Riverside Hospital in Columbus in July. They had become regular visitors to Henry's home out of gratitude for what he had done to help them emigrate to the U.S. But when they discovered that the doctors had not been able to find a kidney donor for him, Kurt sat down by Henry's bed one day.

Kurt's English was excellent, although it still had a slight and attractive German coloring to it. He had never talked seriously with Henry about anything yet, still feeling his way in a new land and a strange relationship. This day, however, he knew that had to change.

"Henry," he told him, "we need to look at things straight on. We are half brothers and that gives us a unique relationship, even though you are thirteen years older. I never knew my father, and you knew him for only the first ten years of your life. But he created a connection between us that means something. So...I am going to have myself tested to see if I am a match for you."

As much as Henry had been involved in the search for a kidney, he had never considered Kurt as a potential donor. There had been too much other work to do, and too much confusion even to think about that possibility. Now, even as he started to protest, he realized that their partial blood relationship might very well facilitate a match.

When the testing was done, much to everyone's enormous relief, Kurt was a perfect match. Their dad had unwittingly created this solution by fathering two boys who both shared his genes, even though they had lived continents apart. The miracle could not have happened, however, without Gerda's conspiracy and Kurt's unselfishness, which in turn was the result of Henry's willingness to overlook his father's indiscretions and accept his half-brother with open arms.

The operation took place in August, before Henry had gotten too sick for it to do him any good. He recovered more quickly than Kurt did, however, because, while the kidney made a sick man better, the donation of that kidney made a well man quite ill for awhile. Henry showed immediate improvement and within two months they were both back to work. Henry bought back into his old practice and went to work with a new sense of gratitude.

Henry's mother was never totally convinced that the whole story was true, but in time she came to tolerate Kurt, in spite of the fact that he looked like a young version of her husband. Kurt's presence was a constant reminder that her husband had been up to no good while he was away at war, and he was certainly no longer anyone's hero.

Although there was little proof of Gerda's story, one small detail was accepted by all of them as irrefutable evidence: the tiny "H" scratched into the bottom of a cheap cigarette lighter by a ten-year-old boy with the tip of his pocket knife.

As for Gerda, she maintained to the end of her days that, when you need a handful of miracles, you should go find someone to smash into your car!

Author's Notes

Thank you for taking the time to read my newest book. It has a very special place in my heart, and I hope you had as much pleasure reading it as I did while writing it.

People ask me where I get the ideas for short stories like these. Well, an author begins with what he knows, and then lets his imagination take over. Obviously, these stories are fictional. But all except one are based on brief memories from my past. Let me share with you the moments of inspiration that generated each one, in the order in which they appear in the book.

The Feather: I once walked along the beach, found a pristine white feather, and gave it to a little girl who was digging in the sand with her mother. I let it go and a breeze off the ocean took it to her. I have often wondered where she is and what she is doing now. I love this story and didn't want it to get lost, so I wrote the book in order to preserve it. And I did say, "Here, you need a feather."

Memories: I have had my own past death recall, which set me on course for a new career. The details of that recall are recorded in two of my non-fiction books. Studying the influence of our past lives can produce significant insights into our current phobias and abilities.

The Key: I once restored a 1942 Chevy Aerosedan, which necessitated going to a local Vo-Tech school to learn how to do auto body work. That's a photo of my car, which I bought for $250 and sold for $1,000 in the 1970's. Ain't she purty?

Merlen: Pure fantasy. I love stories about real mystical events, like this example of after-death communication, of which there are many on record. They show how closely interrelated are the physical and spiritual worlds.

Charlie: Charlie was a real person who was in my grade at Roosevelt School and who lived across the street from the school building. He was one of only two African-American kids in the entire school, and I wonder now what it must have been like for him to be in that all-white school in the 1930's and '40's.

The Voice: I bought a 1950 Chevy Styleline Two-Door Sedan when I graduated from college in 1954. It was a crappy tan color, but I loved it. You always love your first car. I used it to go to graduate school at Princeton Seminary and to visit my girlfriend, Helen, who was a nursing student in Baltimore. We have been married now for 57 years.

The Lighter: I recently had to drive a long detour every day, because the bridge on the only direct road into town was being replaced. There was a right turn in that detour which everyone took. I often wondered if a wreck like the one I describe in the story might some day happen at that intersection.

The Dedication: You might have noticed that I dedicated the book to my four great-grandchildren. I also snuck their names into two of the short stories. You will forgive me if I make use of an author's prerogative and call attention to the exceptional short people in my family.

Contacting me: I would be glad to hear from you. Please feel free to email me at:

john@beyondreligion.com

And please visit our website at:

www.beyondreligion.com